WAYFARER IN THE LAND

HANNAH HURNARD

Tyndale House Publishers, Inc.
Wheaton, Illinois

Library of Congress Catalog Card Number 75-13967
ISBN 8423-7823-5

Published with the permission of
The Church's Ministry Among the Jews
(Olive Press), London, England

United States publications rights secured
by Tyndale House Publishers, Inc.,
Wheaton, Illinois 60187

Third printing, Tyndale edition, January 1976
Printed in the United States of America

CONTENTS

PREFACE

This little book contains the personal experience of one member of a group of Christians, called to the work of going out to try and reach some of the multitude who never come near Christian missions. It was written with the definite aim and prayer, that some who read it may find themselves challenged to engage in the same joyful task, and may find in these pages a few practical and helpful suggestions as to how to set about it.

I have purposely emphasised the weakness and timidity of those who heard the call to launch out into this work, because I think so often when we read the lives of God's great missionaries, we are apt to feel that special and heroic qualities are needed, and that we ourselves are quite unfit for anything more than the daily work we trained for in hospital or school. Certainly there were giants among the missionaries of past generations, and there are today, and reading of their work and wonderful achievements, we may be tempted to feel a little depressed with our own opportunities or abilities.

But it is one of the lovely things about the Master we serve, that He is so willing to use in His service, dwarfs as well as giants, and feeble folk as well as champions. Indeed quite a lot of His work seems to need the feeble and the rather poor material more than the exceptional. And we can all take heart from this. The weak and the foolish things so often seem to be chosen by Him for evangelistic work. Great intellects and outstanding abilities are needed for the work of organising and leading the Church of Christ. But for the simple, daily work of talking to others about the Saviour of the world, you and I by God's grace, may be just the people He needs and can use.

As we have travelled up and down the land during the past ten years, telling of that wonderful wayfaring Man who nearly two thousand years ago passed this way, searching for the lost sheep of the house of Israel, and sent His disciples two and two before His face, to every place whither He Himself would come; we have been radiantly conscious of the unspeakable privilege of following in His steps as He went forth to every town and village.

But, alas, our visits have been so brief, a few hours at most spent in each place seeking to publish the good news, and then we have had to turn away and pass on to other places. The words of Jeremiah 14:8, 9 just seem to describe our feelings. We have seemed to travel with a wayfaring Man, proving that He is in truth the only hope of Israel, their only Saviour in time of trouble. Oh that the day may speedily come when He will be no longer a passing wayfarer, but welcomed into every village and town of His own land, Immanuel's Land, as King and Saviour.

Perhaps there may be some who read this book, who will feel stirred up afresh to pray for all those who are seeking to preach the good news of the living Saviour in lands where He is not known and will claim the quickening power of the Holy Spirit to bring to life in many hearts the Word which the Lord's messengers have sown in weakness and difficulty, and yet with hope. And then together we may rest upon His gracious promise, "So shall My word be that goeth forth out of My mouth, it shall not return unto Me void, but it shall accomplish that . . . whereunto I send it" (Isaiah 55:11).

1
THE WAYFARER'S CALL

"Behold I have set before thee an open door and no man can shut it" (Rev. 3:8).

It was early spring and the beginning of my fifth year on the mission field. In two or three months' time I was due for furlough. We were all gathered in an upper room on the mission compound at Haifa for our weekly staff conference and prayer meeting. Matters for discussion had been dealt with, and special requests for prayer made known, and the time for prayer arrived. I was not dreaming of anything new.

I had not even been specially praying that the door would open for me to launch out into evangelistic work, although when I had first arrived on the mission field it had been with high hopes that I would speedily be able to move out into the villages to undertake direct evangelistic work. But for four years the door had not opened, and shortage of staff, combined with my own inexperience and lack of the necessary language, had barred the way, and it still seemed as though I never would be freed for the special work for which I had felt called. Indeed whenever I thought of such work, I realised my own inadequacy and the great difficulties lying in the way of even attempting the task.

But on this particular morning two of our young men who usually went out each week to a few of the neighbouring Jewish settlements selling Scriptures and giving away tracts, had been reporting on their most recent experiences. And as we bowed in prayer I was still thinking of these special villages they were accustomed to visit, and of course of other settlements in our own district, to which they never went. Then my thoughts turned to the hundreds of other places in neighbouring districts, in some of which no missionary visits were ever made, and where thousands upon thousands of human beings whom Christ Himself had died to redeem, had never heard the message, but lived in deepest darkness.

When it was my turn to pray, I found myself pleading as I had not done for many months past, that the Lord of the Harvest would thrust out labourers who would go into these unreached places and carry the good news.

The circle in that upper room echoed the amen, and then silence fell. And in the silence a strange thing happened. I became aware that our Lord in Whose presence we had gathered, was speaking to me.

With startling clearness He seemed to say, ''The time has come when I am ready to answer that prayer. Are you willing for me to send you? Behold I have set before you an open door, and no man can shut it."

It was an overwhelming moment. The dreadful impossibility of the task swept over me. How could I go? I who spoke so little of the language. Our mission did not approve of women going out alone. I had no companion. There were no means of getting to the more distant villages. And when I got there I would not be able to preach. What did the Lord mean? It was an impossibility He asked. But the words came back again with inescapable insistence, "Behold I have set before thee an open door and no man can shut it." The Lord seemed to say, "I mean to visit these settlements Myself. Will you go with me?"

When we finished prayer I rose with my thoughts in great turmoil, and went out alone into the garden. Pacing one of the terraces under a huge carob tree I faced this extraordinary call. Had I heard the Lord aright? Or was I simply deluding myself? It was true that I had longed and prayed to do evangelistic work, but four years on the mission field had brought me to the place where I felt utterly unfit in every way for the work. I still lacked the necessary language, and there was no one in the mission free to go out with me. And would my senior missionary set me free? And how did one begin such work? And what method should be used? For the call was not to evangelize in our town, but to go out to the unreached places.

As I walked the garden paths I asked the Lord

what method He meant to be used. How should I set about starting such work? There was no experienced worker for me to go out with. I must strike out on my own, I, so weak and cowardly. What should I do when I reached a village? How begin?

And quite clearly it seemed to me the Lord said, "Think back to your years in the Evangelistic Band in England, what method did you follow then? That was your training for the work before you now." And I remembered that our business had been, on arrival in a new village, to visit every house in the place with a personal invitation to the meetings to be held in the church, chapel or mission hall. We were to offer literature to all we met, and to try and get a personal talk about the Lord Jesus Christ, with everyone who came to the door.

Then I said, "But Lord it is quite impossible to do that here in this land. First of all there are no Christian services in the villages to which to invite them, and no Christian place of worship. The law of the land forbids us, uninvited, to hold open-air meetings. So the method used at home is useless here."

And He answered, "Do what you did in every village at home. Go from house to house, and knock on every door, and offer the Word of God to all who can read, and speak to them about Me."

It was overwhelming. I had never heard of such a method in this country to which God had sent me. Our own colporteur would go and sit in cafes and offer his wares there, and sometimes out in the

11

streets and markets. But whoever heard of going from house to house in a Jewish settlement and trying to speak personally to everyone thus met? But even as I thought with horror of such a task, I realized it was practicable. I knew nobody who had done it, but on the other hand, it surely could be done. At least by someone with an adequate amount of Hebrew or other European languages needed!

If only I could speak the language! If only I could understand the people! If only I were a native of the country! But I was only an ineffecient gapfiller with not a single term at language school behind me. And how could I convince my seniors that this was a real call?

But my Lord Himself wanted me to visit these settlements, and had asked me to go with Him. He said He had opened the door and no man could shut it. That must mean that if I would obey, I would find it was possible. And of course if He was going too, that put the whole matter in a very different light. The responsibility and initiative would be His. Even though He would not be visible, He would be as really present as when He had visited the villages with His disciples.

Through all the fear and shrinking in my heart, a sense of amazing privilege began to awaken. I lifted my heart to Him then and there and said yes, I would go with Him. And I asked that He would give me two special signs that I was really understanding His will and not making a mistake. A car, so that we could reach all the settlements in our district, and a companion who would go out with me, for it had been His custom to send His disciples two by two even when He was with them.

I said nothing to anybody for several weeks, but went on praying and claiming the signs and pondering on the task before me, and the method He had called me to follow.

Then a short time before I was due to sail for England, I went to interview our doctor. I told him that I wanted to be set free from the medical work when I came back in the autumn because I believed that God had called me to itinerant work among the Jewish settlements.

The doctor, who for four years had refused to release me, said simply, "Very well. If you have received a clear call and know what God means you to do, you can be free to do it. I hope I may be able to bring another fully trained nurse out with me from England."

I was overjoyed. My senior had agreed to my making the attempt and was prepared to set me free. But what about the car and the fellow worker? How would God meet these needs?

Just at that time a visitor came to see me on her way home for a year's furlough. She was the only person I knew who felt a call to full time evangelistic work. But she lived in quite a different area to the south and though we had both been trained at the same Bible college and had met occasionally at conferences on the field, we were very unlike in temperament and had never been greatly attracted to each other.

However, as her boat sailed from Haifa, where I lived, she came to call. As I knew she was deeply interested in evangelistic work I told her of the call I had received, and my longing to launch out in the autumn. And I asked if she thought there was any chance of our uniting together in this work, for she had years more experience than I had.

I never recall that scene now without a smile. My heart pounding with hope and tensely excited to know if this was the sign that I was in the Lord's way. And her quiet decisive answer, "No, I don't think so, My district is down in the south and yours up here in the north. And I don't think somehow that we are very suited for working together."

I was hurt and disappointed, and yet secretly relieved, for I too felt that we were not by any means a suitable pair. How little we knew that afternoon what God was storing up for us in the future, nor how the time would come when we would recall that conversation with happy laughter; for it was the first link in what developed into the closest possible friendship and love and united service. However, she left for England, and in a few weeks I followed.

But one last thing I did before leaving. I bought a map of the country and very carefully I drew a thick black line all round the boundaries of our own mission district. Every Jewish settlement in that marked off area was my responsibility. There seemed a great number of them. But I paid no attention at all to the many Arab villages in the same area, where the inhabitants spoke another language than the one I was so painfully acquiring, and practised a different religion. I looked at the many settlements in the neighbouring district outside the black line and said firmly, "Those are the responsibility of such and such a mission, and those to the south of another. They are nothing to do with me."

Sometimes I take that old map out and stare at the little marked off section. What would I have said that afternoon if I had known that the Wayfarer Who had called me to follow Him to the Jewish settlements would not rest until every single village in every single district of the whole country had been visited and preached in, and that another difficult language, Arabic, must be tackled as well as Hebrew?

I laugh now at my abysmal ignorance of His plan. I thought the open-door led only to special places in one small area and that seemed a sufficiently preposterous idea. But to Him there are no differences of race and creed. "He had made of one blood all nations of men . . . on all the face of the earth" (Acts 17:26), and His gospel is for all.

Foolish little black mark along the boundary lines! Stupid little messenger with such cramped horizons! The door had been set wide, and though I could dimly see a few of the places into which it opened, I was to find it included the whole land.

2
THE WAYFARER LEADS US OUT

"When He putteth forth His own sheep he goeth before them, and the sheep follow Him" (John 10:4).

When I returned to the mission field in the autumn, I brought back with me a little Baby Austin car, the gift of my father, and the first sign I had asked for was thus granted. But I returned to face the new work before me without the least idea as to who would go out with me to visit the villages in our area.

It so happened that our mission doctor was delayed in England and I returned to the station some weeks before he did. The Mission Sisters therefore were only receiving and treating such patients as did not need the doctor's supervision, and consequently they were much less busy than in the ordinary way.

As soon as I got back and showed them the little car and explained that the doctor had given his full consent to my leaving the medical work and starting visits to the Jewish settlements in our neighborhood, our two beloved Deaconess Sisters were full of interest and delight. They volunteered to go out with me in turn until the return of the doctor made it necessary for both of them to be at the clinics; and thus help me at least to make a start. After that I must wait and see if the Lord would provide anyone else.

This was a great and unexpected joy to me, and I realized that our Sisters who were known to thousands of grateful patients would be the very best companions possible.

Never shall I forget the first day's visiting. Sister Mercy went with me. We determined to visit a little Jewish town only a few miles away built on the sand dunes of Haifa Bay as we knew that quite a number of our patients came from this place. It was wonderful how a loving and understanding Heavenly Father led us first by the easiest possible way, until we were more experienced and better able to meet the difficulties.

We spent a happy and interesting morning visiting the home of our past patients who lived in that hot, sandy, sun-baked little town, where all the streets were shifting sand into which one's feet sank deeply. In nearly every house we read the Scriptures and left literature with such as could read. All of them had had some experience of the little gospel services in our out-patients' department at the mission, and all held the doctor and sisters in grateful remembrance, so that the visiting was comparatively easy and pleasant, even if in some of the homes there did not seem very much interest in our message.

But finally all our patients had been visited, and the afternoon lay before us. We had spent the morning visiting homes where there was already some knowledge of the message we brought. Now we were to go to those who as far as we knew had never been near the mission, and who perhaps had never heard the good news, and who would be prejudiced against us.

First we decided to eat our picnic lunch, and we drove a little way outside the town and sought a patch of shade behind a mimosa hedge. We sat on the dirty, sandy ground, and became strangely silent. Neither of us had ever attempted to go from house to house in a Jewish town before, and the more we thought about it, the more impossible and terrifying it looked.

I still remember vividly the hot, smelly sand, and parched stalks sticking up here and there thickly encrusted with dirty white snails, and how sordid and depressing it all seemed, and the awful feeling that swept over me, that I just could not face the work ahead. I could see that Sister Mercy felt exactly the same. When we had eaten our sandwiches we prayed together. It seemed terribly difficult at that moment to realize the Lord's presence, but certainly He was there, for we both received the strength to get up and start the work which we still felt so unable to do.

We drove slowly back to town, discussing on the way where to begin, as there seemed to be endless hot, sandy streets and we could only visit a certain number of houses in the time before us. Feeling very cowardly and hopelessly weak and foolish we decided to begin at the very first street we came to, and not to penetrate any further. We got out, and carrying our bags of books, approached the first house.

I tapped on the door, and then stood feeling there wasn't a single word I could say when it opened. How should one begin such work at the door of a strange house where the family would be antagonistic to any mention of the Saviour we wanted to speak about?

The door suddenly opened, a head popped out, its owner took one look at our bulging bags and said quickly in Hebrew, "I don't want to buy anything today," and the door was slammed in our faces.

Feeling very crestfallen and terribly conspicuous, we trailed away from that door and approached a second. It was a horrible moment. What idiots we were! How could we ever expect any contact in this way, or get anybody to listen to us at all? Surely the Lord was asking too much of us and this method was not only agonising, but also useless.

As we approached the second house we saw a cobbler's sign outside and turning a corner found the cobbler himself, a little hunchbacked man, sitting in the open doorway, busy at his work. He looked up in surprise at our approach, and then as Sister Mercy bravely held out towards him a little New Testament, he broke into a smile of pleasure and getting up set a bench for us and asked us to sit down. "I have met you before," he said to Sister Mercy, and he told us that he had been a patient years ago in a hospital in one of the great towns of Germany where Sister Mercy had once worked.

How greatly encouraged we were, for we found the impression made on him at that time had been deep and lasting, and he had also wanted to hear more of the gospel but had never had the chance. He listened gladly to Sister Mercy as she with a radiant face poured out her message in her own German language, and he took all the literature we could give and then begged that we would visit him again. That was the very first inkling we had, strange as it now seems, that in this new work we were tackling with such fear and trembling, we would find many souls already prepared and hungry for our message.

It was just like our Father's love and care to lead us to that particular house, and let us glimpse so early on something of the possibilities and opportunities before us.

We stayed as long as possible with this man, unwilling to drag ourselves away and to face the shut doors again; but at last we left and approached a third house. Here Sister Mercy, emboldened by her recent encouragement, knocked, and when the door was opened by a middle-aged women who also spoke German, she smiled in a friendly way and asked if we might have the pleasure of giving her something to read. To our delight we were invited inside the house and were able to sit and speak to her for about a quarter of an hour. She did not seem very interested in what we said, but was frankly curious about us. We left

Scripture portions and other literature in her home, ready for her husband's return in the evening.

We had only time to visit one or two more houses where no special opportunity occurred. But on this first occasion no other door was slammed in our faces and no one refused our books. We were to experience something of that in the future, but on that first day our loving Lord dealt gently with us.

As the evening shadows began to lengthen, we returned to the car and drove home. And we experienced on that very first occasion something which never failed to occur at the end of every day's village visiting. A joy filled our hearts—a joy extraordinarily radiant and quite unlike anything experienced at other times. All day we had been burdened and timid and often frankly frightened. Now we laughed and sang and rejoiced together all the way home. It was always the same on every future occasion. No matter how depressing and discouraging the visiting might have seemed at the time, whenever we sat down to rest afterwards, or turned our faces homeward, the Great Shepherd always gave us this peculiarly radiant joy.

The second visit which was made in the company of Sister Patience, was to a small isolated settlement at the foot of a lonely hill. Most of the dwellings were miserable, ramshackle huts, and the village which had been attacked some few months earlier by raiders from a neighbouring Arab village, had a half-ruined and very desolate aspect. We found that many of the inhabitants had left the village altogether, and their deserted houses added to the derelict appearance of the place. Those who remained were inclined to be very orthodox and fanatical in their religious beliefs, and it is probable that at any other time our house to house visits would have been difficult and perhaps actively opposed.

But on this occasion we found several poverty striken homes whose owners seemed glad of a chance to pour out the story of their hardships, and of the attack launched upon them, and were grateful for a sympathetic hearing. We had therefore an unexpectedly good opening, and once again we found that if we waited on God for guidance, He could be trusted to lead us to places that had already been prepared for our coming.

One special thing I remember about this occasion. As we sat down to eat our lunch in one of the half-ruined, empty huts on the outskirts of the village, an armed Jewish watchman passed by. He stared at us in some surprise, as most people did on such occasions; two lonely foreign women wandering about together in such troublous times, for the 1936 Arab riots were just starting, being an unusual sight in the country places; then he came up to speak to us.

Sister Patience wore her distinctive Deaconess uniform, and after staring at us for a moment, this young watchman said in a friendly tone of voice "You must be missionaries. Have you any Christian literature I can read?" And once again we found a soul who had been brought into touch with Christians in the past and was glad to hear more about their Lord.

We found this unaccustomed work of visiting in the villages extremely tiring, all the more so because we had to experiment all the time in order to find the best way of setting about it. But very quickly we got into the habit of waiting upon God, before ever we went out, for His guidance as to which village He would have us visit. We did not work out a methodical plan, and after crossing out each place visited, say, "this is the next on our list we will go there next time," but we spread the survey map out before us and studied the different names and positions of the places and then definitely asked that we might be led to real assurance as to which we were to visit next.

Also whenever we went out we used to stop the car some distance away from the place we were going to, for prayer, and in order to claim that the door would be open for us, and that we might be led to individuals whose hearts had already been prepared in some way.

I mention this because experience has led me to believe that this is a more practical and successful way of going about such work, than a cut and dried plan however methodically it may be prepared. It is better to trust the Holy Spirit to lead us to those He knows are ready for our coming, than to parcel out a village, so many houses to be visited and so many streets to be finished in a certain time. Also it seems to me that in such work we should be very adaptable and ready to modify or change at a moment's notice any part of the arrangement, as the Holy Spirit may prompt, rather than to insist on adhering rigidly to the original plan.

Often we have driven slowly right through a village, praying that the Lord would make us sure which street to stop in, and have perhaps turned back and retraced our steps to one special street and there found a particularly needy soul awaiting us. And we have been amazed at the many hungry, dissatisfied hearts with which we came in contact, and the many who through recent sorrow, bereavement, illness, or other family troubles, were conscious of their need of some refuge and of more than human help.

Another point which we also made a special matter for prayer, was that the Lord would make us more skilful in winning the interest and confidence of the people as soon as the door was opened, so that we might get inside the house and have the opportunity for a real talk, undisturbed by the curious stares of passers-by. It seemed to us that a few really earnest talks inside a house, when individuals would speak to us of their own religious experience, or complete lack of it, and confess their deepest needs, was far more worth while than scattering literature at a far larger number of houses, though that is very worth while work too.

We prayed earnestly therefore that we might develop a better technique of approach, and we found that far the most likely means of being invited into a house was a friendly smile and a courteous and kind greeting, and some appreciative remark if possible, about the garden or the building, or a sympathetic enquiry about obvious difficulties, such as the lack of water, miserable condition of the road, or lonely situation of the village. We learnt to keep on the alert for points of friendly contact, and have come to feel pretty certain that a stiff, reserved manner, or dogmatic patronising tone of voice, will bar the door quicker than anything else, while a friendly smile and easy natural greeting will often effect wonders.

I am not of course forgetting that an easy natural manner is the one thing the novice at such work feels that she is never likely to acquire, but the fact is, as we have seen again and again, the shyest and most awkward can achieve it as a result of humble, believing prayer, and an earnest desire to forget oneself altogether, and to think only of the need and spiritual poverty of those being visited.

On the other hand it may be necessary later on to keep a sharp check on oneself in order to avoid going to the opposite extreme, and rushing into insincere gushing or flattery. This can be a very real snare, as I well remember discovering on one occasion when we were trying to get into the house of a very fanatical old lady, whose cottage was in a terribly neglected and dirty condition.

She was pouring out a torrent of abuse against us, and while this was going on, I noticed a particularly ugly and crude piece of embroidery hanging on the wall just inside the door, and when she paused for breath, I said, as sweetly as possible (being loth to turn away unsuccessful), "What a beautiful piece of embroidery you have there. I wonder if I may be allowed to look at it."

Far from being mollified however, she swung around on me and shouted, "Now don't you try to get round me in that way you hypocrite! You know as well as I do that you are not the least interested in it." I knew this thoroughly served me right, and felt very properly rebuked.

I mention all these points in passing, as we ourselves learned everything in the hard school of experience, and passed through many stages of experiment and lack of success. We discovered pitfalls by falling into them, and came to realize the better ways of approach only after sorrowing over bad ones. But there is no reason why other novices at such work, warned by our experience, should not avoid these mistakes from the very beginning.

When the doctor returned in a few weeks time, the Sisters were no longer able to go out. But a young Hebrew Christian woman offered to be my companion. She had an extremely gentle and pleasant manner which proved very disarming, and as she also had the two main languages, German and Hebrew, it was quite ideal. We visited together in the truest harmony and divided the work in the following way.

It was my business to knock on the door and gain the interest of whoever answered it, (a not very easy task to one ill-equipped with very faulty German and Hebrew, though such work as this quickly developed greater fluency), and then when an entry had been effected, it was the part of Peace with her fluent language, to carry on the conversation and to do the preaching. As she was rather shy and very gentle, she did not find the opening work easy. But once we were inside the house her timidity disappeared, and her whole face glowed with earnestness and loving interest as she opened all her heart and poured forth the message of the Saviour's love.

As she herself was a convert, she often had to undergo a good deal of reproach and scorn, but she was never unduly distressed by this and gave the reasons for her change of faith with such simple and direct earnestness so that she had a far better opportunity than any which could have come my way. She became indeed an ideal companion and it was wonderful to watch the growing boldness and joy with which she did this work. We were both learning to love it however, though we suffered a great deal of nervousness and dread before each visit, which for a very long time never seemed to get any less. But we practised together, and were always on the look-out for better ways of establishing contact.

Peace's great gift was that she never let her message become cut and dried, but adapted it to every individual case. Since those days I have been out with not a few people who felt they had to make certain statements of doctrine, and quote certain texts, and that the sooner these could be introduced, the better, and then their work was done and their message safely delivered. They never waited to get to know or sense the spiritual condition of those they were speaking to. But Peace always tried to get those we were visiting to speak quite freely, and to tell us as much as they would about their own religious beliefs, and then she would follow on from that with a message which "Spoke to their condition," as the Quakers express it.

It seems impossible to emphasize too much how tremendously important this is, and how sadly useless it can be if one gets into a stereotyped way of quoting texts and concentrating on certain doctrines, a habit which one can fall into quite easily. It is like trying to fix on a patch of the wrong colour and material, and unsuitable in every way.

I do not mean of course that it does not matter if the heart of the gospel message is left out altogether, but that our message is likely to prove useless to many hearers unless they can first be helped to feel their need of it. This cannot be done by quoting texts which we think ought to convict them, but by first coming to understand their spiritual condition, and then seeking to lead them to see in what ways it is inadequate. Every individual soul differs in spiritual experience even though they may all be adherents of one particular religion.

3
THE WAYFARER TEACHES US TO FISH FOR MEN

"Jesus said unto them 'Come ye after me and I will make you to become fishers of men'" (Mark 1:17).

We plodded on steadily at our job, going two or three days each week, until gradually we had visited most of the settlements in our area. The more difficult ones we left till the last, that is to say, the places with particularly rough tracks, and those which we knew by repute to be exceptionally orthodox. Although in one sense the work never became any easier, and we suffered the same nervousness and shrinking before each visit, our interest and enjoyment in it increased steadily. We were very conscious, weak and foolish though we were, of our Lord's presence with us in a way we had seldom before experienced.

Especially was this the case on the very frequent occasions when it was difficult for the little car to get to the villages. For though in those early days were only visiting villages comparatively easy to reach, my experience of driving in England had not prepared me for tackling the appalling sandy wastes and rocky mountain tracks which we had now to cope with every time we left the main road. I lived even then in constant dread of the car breaking down or getting stuck in some remote place where there would be no one to help us. It was well indeed that at that time I did not foresee the kind of driving I should be called upon to tackle in the future.

We knew that a great deal of the inland plain behind Haifa became a bog in the rainy season, but as soon as the finer weather appeared, and the brief loveliness of the green and flowered earth began to change to yellow and brown, I supposed that the tracks across the plain to a group of settlements in a green oasis would be dry enough for us to make the attempt to visit them. Three times over we tried, but always saw bog ahead and had to turn back.

Finally, one lovely, fine, sunny day, we decided on a further effort, and this time found the narrow camel track comparatively firm, although of course painfully bumpy. We were drawing much nearer to the group of houses than we had managed before, and just then we met two Jews with mules, ploughing a desolate patch of ground. We stopped and asked if it were possible to drive the whole way to the first village and were assured that the ground was now firm enough if we were careful, but the men did shout some remark after us as we drove off, which we did not catch.

Evidently it was a last minute instruction to leave the beaten track a little further on, but it came too late, for within a few minutes, with no warning at all, we sank into a tremendous 'slough of despond' and the car settled far down in the mud and became immovable, just as Sisera's chariots long ago sank in this same boggy land and lost their wheels.

A terrible feeling of complete helplessness swept over me, and a panicky fear that our precious new car must remain there for ever, gradually sinking lower and lower in the slough till it disappeared altogether.

However, panic was the very last thing we could afford to indulge in at that moment, and we gingerly opened the doors and stepped out. Instantly both large, serviceable village shoes were sucked off my feet, and were with difficulty retrieved. Carrying them and the more precious of our possessions, we waded and squelched to firmer ground, and woefully made our way back to the men with the mules, who morosely asked us why we had been so self-willed and had not heeded their warning.

They agreed, however, to unhitch the mules from the plough and attempt a piece of rescue work. But the mules were terrified at the bog and plunged and kicked and reared, and it soon became evident that they never could be got near enough to be hitched on to our pathetic little car. We were therefore advised to walk the remaining distance to the nearest settlement, which, it seemed, possessed a communal tractor which might or might not be available.

So we set out forlornly, the mud drying and caking on

our legs, and as we went we prayed that the Lord who had called us out to visit this village, would in some way rescue the car. We carried our bags of books with us as I did not relish the idea of making the attempt again, even if the car could be extracted. So we plodded on across the plain, the long range of Carmel behind and to our right Mount Tabor, reminding us of the fame of Deborah and Barak, and Sisera's warriors of long ago, trapped by this self-same bog!

Eventually we reached the village and enquired about the tractor. The first answer to our prayers was the discovery that the tractor was actually in the village and not out in any of the fields, and the drivers agreed to attempt the rescue. They said it would take an hour at least to get the tractor ready and back across the plain to where the car was bogged, and so we decided to utilise part of that time in visiting from door to door in the village, and as we were able to move much more quickly than the tractor, we could overtake it later on.

It was not easy work going round from house to house, for besides being thickly caked with mud, we were both depressed and anxious about the car and wondering how we should get home if it remained immovable. However, we went round to most of the houses in that tiny settlement and gave away a fair amount of literature in many different languages and then hurried off in the wake of the tractor.

Finally we arrived at the bog in which our precious car was trapped. The tractor wormed its way forward. It was quite one of the worst moments we had experienced since starting the visiting work, when the tractor itself as it reached the little car also sank and refused to budge an inch.

The men shouted at one another desperately and the engine roared, but nothing happened, for the wheels just turned round and round and found no grip. A feeling of great despair clutched us, and unable to bear the sight any long, Peace and I turned our backs on the car and did the only thing left to us at that painful moment. We began to pray aloud for help.

Suddenly the men on the tractor shouted triumphantly. The wheels had gripped, and inch by inch they squirmed out of the bog on to firmer ground, and then made their way towards the back of the car, which by this time seemed to have sunk even deeper. A chain was then attached to the back axle and the tractor attempted to back. At first nothing happened, then there was a great sucking squelch and the baby car began to lift and respond to the pull.

In a few minutes we were almost dancing with joy as we beheld it once more on firm ground. But what a spectacle. The lower half of the car from end to end was encased in thick black mud, and the wheels of course would not grip. We all seized whatever we could lay our hands on from the tool box, and began scraping the wheels and dislodging huge chunks of mud from the under-parts of the car, and at long last, in the late afternoon, we were able to bump thankfully back along the camel track to the safety of the main road, very plentifully besmeared with evidences of our recent adventure.

We were soon faced with a new challenge to faith, and a job which both of us shrank from in real fear. A large village remained unvisited in our area, where the people were notably more orthodox than any others, and belonged to the strictest sect of their religion. We would gladly have missed this place out altogether, but the more we prayed about it, the more clearly the answer seemed to come, "Go preach the gospel to every creature," and the need must include the orthodox and fanatical as well as the more easy-going.

The day came when all the villages had been reached except this one, and two or three others, which as I shall explain later, seemed even more formidable and alarming than the one before us.

I can still remember the ghastly feeling, somewhere in the pit of my stomach, as we approached the side road which would lead us to this orthodox settlement. Quite automatically I decreased speed until we were only crawling along. Neither of us spoke a word. I dared not tell Peace how frightened I was for fear of making her feel worse, and she was silent for the same reason.

We stopped the car just outside the village and had our usual time of prayer, and then as the inevitable must be faced, we started off again and drove into the village. Here I was so literally inhibited by fright that I could not stop the car, and we drove straight through the large village and out again on the other side, and only came to a standstill when all the houses were left behind.

So we had some more prayer and turned round and drove into the village again, and as good as repeated the manoeuvre, only just as we were crawling out on the first side we had entered by, Peace said "Let's turn left up this street where there are only a few houses, and start there." This we did, but even so I drove right along the street without stopping and only the fact that it proved to be a blind alley, prevented us from leaving the village in yet a third direction. When at last the road came to an abrupt end, we stopped and climbed out.

I have only a confused recollection of what happened then. Evidently our initial entry into the village, and departure, and mysterious return, had aroused interest. Also some boys quickly gathered round the car and spotted our bags of books. They enquired who we were and why we had come, and, despair making us bold, we answered with the bald statement that we were Christian missionaries and had brought literature with us. Whereupon, though we were too nervous to notice it, the little boys dispersed in all directions.

We then made our way up to the first house, and a man wearing the traditional garments indicating his strict orthodoxy, met us at the door. As we stood talking to him and showing our books, the astounding thing happened. People began hurrying towards us from all directions, and as they came up they clamoured for our books and Scripture portions. Again and again we explained that we were Christians and these were Christian books, and still they clamoured. Then Peace, unable to restrain her astonishment said, "But I thought you were all very orthodox Jews. Why do you want these books about the Christ?"

And somebody answered immediately, "Outwardly we are orthodox, but inwardly we are dissatisfied."

One special person stands out in my hazy memory of that three-quarters of an hour. A very frail old man painfully pushed his way through the crowd and clutched my arm. "Give me one of those books" he quavered, and pointed to the last Hebrew New Testament which remained, and for which so many were clamouring that I did not know whom to choose. He was old and pathetically frail, and my heart smote me. All his long life evidently he had lived according to the strictest traditions of his religion. Now he surely could not understand what he was asking for. If he took this book into his hands he would be defiled.

He had always supposed that it was a blasphemous book and that he should spit at every mention of the One about whom it spoke. How could I let him unwittingly touch a book by which he would afterwards feel that he had been made unclean. He plucked my arm again beseechingly, and I said as gently as possible, "I think perhaps you do not know what this book is. It is the New Testament, and is all about Jesus, the Christ."

"Yes, yes," he said impatiently, "I understand that. For many years I have wanted to read this book, but never found a copy." And as I placed it in his hand he opened it and held it under his short-sighted eyes and without a word turned away, reading as he went, and taking no further notice of anyone.

Meanwhile the crowd increased. We could only knock on two or three doors, and were then kept busy giving literature to all who hurried up to us.

In a very short time every Testament and Scripture portion we had brought with us had been given away. Our bags were empty, and feeling quite overwhelmed, we turned to leave, as it looked as though the whole settlement would soon flock out and trouble be stirred up. As we pushed our way to the car, people from other streets who had only just arrived and had not succeeded in getting books, begged that we would return and bring more with us, very specially a supply of New Testaments.

Feeling quite dazed and wondering if we were in a dream we drove out of the village, and then drew up at the side of the road to discuss the matter. We could hardly believe it was true. What ought we to do about it? We felt completely unable to deal with the situation, and as we finally turned homeward, we decided that we must make a return visit the following week, with more literature and the New Testaments they had asked for, and also that we would beg a certain earnest Christian gentleman from our town to go with us and make the very most of an opportunity which we felt too inefficient and weak to deal with alone.

Accordingly the following week, three of us went back to this place. As soon as we entered the village we were recognized, and it become obvious at once that hostile influences had been at work during the interval. Crowds gathered in the street again, many still eager for literature, but many others bent on thwarting our visit. They had evidently been organized and prepared for our coming, especially the boys of the village, and we found that an uproar was imminent. Those who wanted literature became afraid of showing their interest, and withdrew, and only the unruly element remained, mobbing round the car and shouting insults.

The friend we had brought with us suggested that we drive to the house of the Rabbi and try to get a talk with him and calm matters down. This we did, the unruly mob pressing round the car and going with us.

The Rabbi came to his door and tried to speak, but there was too much noise for us to be able to talk, and he beckoned us into the house. He was very courteous and quite willing to discuss the object of our visit, if he could have had the opportunity of doing so. But the crowd of young hooligans outside, shouted and battered on the door, and yelled through the windows, "Turn them out." "Why do you let Christians into your house? What have they come for? What are they saying to you? It is a shame for you to speak to them."

Stones began to rattle on the roof and walls, and although the Rabbi went to the door and tried to still the rabble, we found that all the responsible adults had left, and only the boys remained. They paid no heed to his request that they should disperse, and it was quite obvious that a quiet talk would be impossible.

As it was plain there was no opportunity for us to visit quietly from house to house, I decided that I would try and draw off the crowd of boys, and leave Peace and our friend to talk with the Rabbi. So I opened the door and slipped out, and as an instant's hush fell, I said with a cheerfulness which I was far from feeling, that if they would follow me I would be glad to answer any questions about ourselves and the purpose of our visit, that they cared to ask. To my great relief the ruse succeeded. They closed in around me, evidently glad to have a visible target for their abuse, and I led the way to an open grassy slope just outside the Rabbi's garden, in sight of the house and car, but far enough away to ensure comparative quiet for the friends inside the house.

I sat down on a rock, and about twenty boys between the ages of eight and sixteen gathered around. They began shouting questions at me, but as I was quite miraculously able to maintain a quiet and smiling demeanour, they very quickly quieted down. First they plied me with a lot of simple questions about their Torah, and seemed surprised when I answered them all correctly, and thus revealed a knowledge of the book quite unexpected in a Christian.

Somewhat mollified, they quieted still more. Then one of them picked up a large stone and announced that he was going to smash my watch, as their holy book said that all unbelievers were accursed and should be treated as badly as possible. I replied with surprise that in a careful study of their book I had never come across any such statement, but on the contrary, I thought they were exhorted to show courtesy and hospitality to strangers who sought their help and protection and to follow the example of their father Abraham. I asked him to give me chapter and verse in support of his statement, and everybody laughed and he sheepishly dropped the stone.

But they were not yet satisfied. One of them pointed to a stone lying on the ground and said, "That's your God, you Christians worship stones." Another cried out "No, this is their God," and placed two sticks on the ground in the shape of a cross, and then ground his heel on the sticks and spat. And yet a third laughed and pointed to a village dog, slinking on the outskirts of the crowd, and shouted, "No, their God is a dog, look at him over there."

A curious thing happened as I sat there on the rock, listening to their mockery and looking at their laughing faces. The inner nervousness all went and a quite unexpected surge of longing and a desire to help them filled me. The ringleader who had done most of the catechising, was about fourteen years old, with black hair and alert, flashing eyes, and a bold, easy way of quelling the others, when he wanted to speak himself. As I watched him so eagerly standing up for his own religion, and trying to demonstrate the badness of mine, I was reminded of young Saul of Tarsus, and then I pictured this boy as a disciple of Jesus Christ, and just as earnestly defending his faith in Him.

And then the crowd of faces all staring at me no longer belonged to a rabble of hooligans, but to a crowd of Jewish boys who had never once had the opportunity of hearing about the Saviour. And who could say when they would hear if I said nothing now. I pictured the Lord Jesus Himself sitting on the rock and talking to them in His own wonderful way, and how quickly He would have won them. And then I lifted my heart in an earnest prayer that He would take my mouth and mind and say something to them through me.

Then I said haltingly in Hebrew and groping for the right words, "No, the God I worship is not a stone, nor a cross of wood, nor a dog. Let me tell you a little about Him."

I think they must have sensed how earnestly I wanted to tell them for they hushed and listened, and even helped me out with the Hebrew words when I got stuck, and though it was desperately little that I could say, they grew very friendly, and at last asked me for some portions of the Scriptures. I smiled and said "I am afraid you will tear them up."

But the ringleader said, "No, give them to me. I know who will read them and who will tear them."

I handed him a gospel, and two or three voices shouted, "Tear it up"—"It's vile," but he thrust it under his ragged shirt, and smiled at me

41

reassuringly, and said "Don't be afraid, I won't tear it or let anyone else do so."

When the door of the Rabbi's house opened and my friends came out, we were allowed to drive quietly away. We went to the other side of the village, and tried to visit there, but after speaking at only one or two houses, the crowd began to collect again, incited by a handful of would-be disturbers, and so we decided to leave.

We had learnt another important lesson. Leave plenty of time in between visits, especially if there has been unusual response and interest, for the enemy will at once try to stir up opposition ready for the next visit. Whereas if a longish period is allowed to elapse the opposition may die down from lack of fuel and lack of opportunity to express itself.

Over and over again later experience confirmed the wisdom of this. Visits repeated too soon were nearly always difficult, and perhaps were thwarted by active opposition, but visits repeated after the lapse of some months were often times of special blessing and particularly good reception. Those who had been truly interested at the first visit were able to hear more, and were not so fearful of seeking us out.

Only two settlements in our district now remained unvisited. But they required quite a different kind of approach. The inhabitants lived a communal life, and did not have private homes. How then could we contact them individually? There was no possibility of going from house to house because they lived in large buildings altogether, and during the day-time men and women were out working in the fields.

Peace and I were at our wits end to know what we should do when we arrived, and how to tackle the job. By this time we were more accustomed to going from door to door, but what could one do in a place where everyone herded together?

We reached the first communal settlement after a difficult journey, in the middle of the morning, and it seemed more or less deserted, as most of the inhabitants were out in the fields and gardens. It was surrounded by a protective stockade, a sad necessity for all new Jewish settlements from 1936 onwards. We met one or two men near the gate and shyly spoke to them and offered literature which they accepted suspiciously, but they did not ask us into the settlement. We felt unable to penetrate further and knock on the doors of any of the big buildings, and so we turned sorrowfully away wondering if there was any possible method of gaining entrance into such places as these.

It was mid-day when we approached the second settlement and we found the young men and women streaming home from the fields for a mid-day meal and rest. We stopped the car and speaking to one man, shyly asked if we might visit the settlement. He seemed surprised but hospitably invited us to accompany him to the communal dining room and share their meal, and then he would show us anything we were interested to see.

Feeling very strange and awkward,

clutching our bags, we followed him into a large hot barrack of a room, full of flies. There were a number of bare wooden trestle tables and benches, and already these benches were full of hot, perspiring men and women, hurriedly gulping down their food. A basketful of thick hunks of course bread stood in the centre of each table, also a jar of discoloured spoons and forks. This was a pioneer settlement; few houses were as yet built, and they were still living a hard primitive life with the barest necessities.

Bowls of steaming vegetable soup were set before us, our guide grabbed a hunk of bread and a spoon, and we did likewise. I had never in my life imagined so many flies, they settled in thick layers all over the table, food, and windows, and their buzzing made loud background to the conversation.

We were far too nervous and ill at ease in these unaccustomed surroundings to speak to anybody at our table, and we sat awkwardly gulping down our food. As soon as the meal was finished the room emptied and our guide asked if we cared to see around the settlement. We assented gratefully and followed him on a tour of inspection of the gardens and fields they were so toilsomely wresting from the barren rock-strewn wilderness, and then we returned to the car.

All this time we had never spoken one word as to the reason of our visit, and now, shamefaced and miserable, we explained to our guide that we were missionaries and would like to leave some literature. His manner changed at once, and much abashed we realized that we had been accepting hospitality under false pretences. I do not know when I have felt more ashamed and wretched. We had taken up his meagre spare time and been offered a meal, while all the time he was in complete ignorance of the purpose of our visit. He accepted the New Testament in rather a surly manner and left abruptly, and that was all we managed to leave in that place.

Feeling quite exhausted, and with a sense of having failed in a despicable manner and all because of cowardice, we drove away and hid ourselves in a quiet spot and talked over the whole miserable business. We had failed because we had been too cowardly to speak openly and honestly.

And then and there, as we confessed this failure to the Lord, I registered a vow that on all future occasions when visiting this kind of communal settlement we would honestly explain at the very beginning who we were and why we had come, so that, even if we were then unable to find any entry at all, we should at least have lifted up the standard of our Lord, and there would be no danger of going under false colours, or of bearing no witness at all.

But then how would it ever prove possible to gain an entrance into such difficult places, and how should we be able to contact the inhabitants? I remembered again the promise I had been given, and which had been so wonderfully fulfilled in all the other places: "Behold I have set before thee an open door and no man can shut it." Then there must surely be some way of getting into them which the

Lord Himself could be trusted to show us.

As we sat praying and talking together, we ourselves could think of no method at all by which we could obtain real contact with the people in such colonies, we could only pray that the wayfaring Saviour Himself would teach us and open the door just as He had promised when He gave the call.

We did realize two outstanding things however from this first attempt which had seemed such a failure. First, that the Lord's messengers must be prepared to show their colours courageously, or no witness could be given. And secondly, that quite obviously the only times for contacting the inhabitants of such places was during the mid-day meal hour, or in the evening after their work was finished. Neither of these conclusions was very comforting to timid people, and the mere thought of attempting to penetrate to another such dining-room was agonising.

4
THE WAYFARER'S FELLOW LABOURERS

"For His name's sake they went forth" (III John 7).

In a few months we were able to mark off the last names on our map, within the black enclosing boundary lines of the area for which we thought our mission was responsible. Every place had been visited at least once.

But by that time the black boundary line which I had made several months before, had already begun to look ridiculous. The work had proved wonderfully fascinating and encouraging. It filled my thoughts completely. And there were all those settlements to the east and south of us. Careful enquiry had revealed the fact that missions in those areas were too busy and understaffed to undertake outside work in more than a handful of places. Many scores of Jewish settlements in the country still remained unreached. How much longer must they wait?

Peace was just about to be married and would no longer be free to join me in the work. I went over and over again the names of the many more places to the south of us. As I prayed and waited on the Lord for guidance, He showed the next vitally important step.

If those settlements were to be reached, I must seek the co-operation of the missionaries in that area. So I wrote to a missionary in Tel Aviv telling of the burden on my heart for these unvisited places, and asked if they would be willing for me to stay at their mission station, and if I supplied the literature and means of transport, would it be possible for some of them to take it in turns to go out with me three or four days each week? The answer came back, welcoming me there, and saying that they would see what could be done.

Thus began the first step in co-operating with other missions, the best way surely for doing such work. To trespass uninvited in areas worked by others, is discourteous and wasteful overlapping. To co-operate together, each one contributing some vital part of the necessary equipment, is joy and power. And provided there is mutual interest in the work and oneness of aim, namely to preach the gospel to those who have not heard it, such co-operation can bring unimagined joys of new friendships, of Christian fellowship, and enlarged horizons.

Perhaps nothing so unites people of varying temperament and outlook, as sharing together in this work of going out to seek the lost sheep. Differences of doctrinal belief or methods of church government simply do not come into this work. The aim is to preach the good news to those who do not come to the churches to hear it, and when this great urge fills the heart, the things that divide get laid aside. The personal enrichment and help which has come to me as the result of such co-operation, is one of the greatest joys of the work. And I believe that to share in direct evangelism with members of other denominations, probably helps on the ecumenical ideal more than anything else.

It was a great joy to find so many fellow helpers ready and able to go out on these next trips. Three or four different missions took part, their workers giving one day a week, and the friend with whom I was staying usually went out with us twice a week, so that we never lacked helpers.

It was intensely interesting to watch the different methods and ways of approach, used by the different members of this group. None of them had done house to house work before, so that it was still largely experimental. I was terribly keen to learn new and better ways of approach, and used to watch fascinated, the different technique gradually evolved by my companions. One and all at this stage of the work, shrank from announcing at the beginning that we were missionaries, as that word was held in great abhorrence by the Jewish people, and it was feared that the doors would close at once if we gave ourselves away too soon.

The general idea was that it was better to show a friendly, non-committal manner, and attempt to arouse the curiosity of those who came to the door, and not to show our hand until we had been asked into the house. But I was constantly haunted by the bitter memory of our failure in the communal settlements in our district, and the vow that we had made that we would always show our colours fearlessly. So that gradually we began announcing the fact that we were missionaries as the door was opened.

Often as we had feared and expected, an expression of angry annoyance would appear on the face of whoever had answered our knock, and it would look as though the door would be closed at once. But when this happened we would hurry on to say with a friendly smile, "Perhaps you are one of those people who don't like missionaries?"

And this often seemed to have a disarming effect. As often as not the answer would be "Yes, I am. I think missionaries are busybodies who would be much better attending to their own business and leaving us alone to worship God in the way we think best and right. What right have you to come and try to make us change our religion? Far better go and preach to your own Christian people and try and make them better. When you have converted Hitler and the Nazis we shall be more willing to listen. And look how Christians quarrel and fight and persecute. Go to them first and don't interfere with us until you have a better type of Christianity to show."

This at least gave us a good conversational opening, and it was easy to go on and say more on the subject, adding, "But you see we only come because we do feel that we have a tremendously important message, and as we have come so far to visit you, I wonder if you would be so kind as to let us come inside and tell you why we think it is so important."

Thus even if the confession that we were missionaries sometimes provoked resentment at first, it did, nearly always, open the way for a free discussion of the matter which we felt so important. But surprisingly often it had quite a different effect, and the friendly announcement that we were missionaries, would bring a smile of pleasure or interest and a cordial welcome to enter, followed by the remark, "I was a patient in such and such a missions hospital" or "I went to mission school. Please come inside." So that I, personally, became more and more convinced that the wisest and the most successful method was to take the bull by the horns at the very outset, and I have stuck to this method ever since.

Everybody who does this kind of work, naturally evolves their own method, and I mention these different things merely as a matter of interest and as pointers to different avenues of approach. It is of the greatest value to notice different methods and to gather as much useful help as possible.

When once the door was opened, methods of giving the message also varied very interestingly.

There was the preacher who loved to get in as much of the Scriptures and the plan of salvation as possible. I remember sitting with him in one little house listening to him start off in Genesis, sweep majestically through the Law of

Moses and the Prophets, on through the Gospels, the coming of Christ, His death and resurrection, then through the Acts of the Apostles, a brief summary of the chief doctrines from some of the Epistles, and ending up triumphantly in Revelation, with the second coming of Christ. All this within the compass of less than half an hour.

And I must do him the justice to say that the young couple in whose house we were sitting, made no attempt to interrupt, though I thought, possibly erroneously, that there was a slightly dazed expression on their faces at the end.

Others based all their effort on proof texts and the Bible prophecies. This of course may be good if you happen to be talking to someone who knows and believes the Old Testament, but when dealing with young modern people who never read the Bible and are not interested in the Law, or look upon the teaching of Carl Marx as sacred, this method of approach does not prove very convincing.

The missionary with whom I was staying was really excellent at this kind of work. She was ready to do some sympathetic listening, as well as witnessing, and after listening to some tale of sorrow or trouble she would point out quietly and earnestly how God alone, and not a human being, can help in such times of need, and how in Jesus Christ, God Himself has come near us in order to be the Helper and Saviour we need. Encouraging receptions were at least as numerous as violent opposition. Polite indifference was our hardest obstacle.

5
THE
WAYFARER'S LOVE

"Though I speak with the tongues of men and of angels, and have not Love, I am become as sounding brass and a tinkling cymbal" (I Cor. 13:1).

About this time, a friend in Jerusalem who had heard of the visits we had been making to the villages, wrote to say that for a long time she had wanted to visit a group of Jewish pioneer settlements in the Jordan Valley in the wildest part of the country, and before leaving for her home country she longed to fulfil this desire, as the doctor had told her that very probably she would be unable ever to return.

These settlements which were so much on her heart, had been established in hitherto uncultivated areas almost entirely peopled by wandering Bedouin tribes, and the settlers were forced to endure great hardships of every kind, as they began their task of wringing a living out of the undeveloped land. It was also a very hot and malarious district, a part of the Jordan Valley being the lowest spot on the earth's surface.

At
that time there were no roads anywhere, and the
tribes themselves were noted for their fierce, unruly behaviour. They were constantly quarrelling
and fighting with one another, and often attacked
the settlements. Murder was common, and so was
highway robbery, and political unrest added further tension and danger to the situation.

My heart
sank despairingly when my friend wrote to ask if I
would accompany her on a trip to these wild
places, myself to provide the car and act as chauffeur, and she to do the preaching. It seemed a very
alarming task to contemplate, and I knew that the
mission hospitals on the borders of that district
were constantly treating the people for malignant
malaria and typhoid, not to mention gun-shot
wounds and still more frequent stabbings.

Yet
there were no missionaries living in the whole area,
except two ladies pioneering in a little town in the
heart of the district, and it was quite obvious that
this was one of the really unreached places where
the good news ought to be taken.

We could not go
to the tribesmen, as neither my friend nor I could
speak a word of their language; but to the pioneer
settlers we surely ought to go. I felt it was a real
call and challenge, but I also felt I simply could not
face it. I remember turning to the Lord in despair
and saying "Please Lord Jesus, don't ask me to go,
I am so afraid. Send somebody braver." And it
seemed to me that very gently and clearly He
asked: "What is it you are afraid of, Grace?" And I

named out loud to Him the whole list of scarecrows.

"There are no roads and no garages, and I am afraid of the car breaking down with no one to repair it, and of being stranded in the wilds without help. I am afraid of getting malaria or typhoid, or probably both. And I am afraid of being shot, or attacked by the tribesmen." And last of all, and very shamefacedly I mentioned it, "I am not willing to face the heat and discomfort and to sleep in those uncomfortable settlements."

And quite clearly it seemed to me that He answered, "If you will go with Me, and face whatever discomfort and weariness there may be on this trip, I promise you that the car will not break down, that you will not get malaria or typhoid, and you will not be shot, nor hurt, nor molested in any way."

The assurance seemed so vivid and real that I immediately wrote it down in a little notebook kept for such purposes, and then wrote off to tell my friend that I would go with her. I thought of Boreham's lovely little essay on *Scarecrows*, an essay which this particular "Miss Much Afraid" frequently takes out and re-reads.

He tells us that there are only two kinds of birds, the wise and the foolish. The foolish are afraid of scarecrows. The wise know that wherever a scarecrow is to be seen, the richest and choicest fruits are to be found also, for no bird ever found a scarecrow planted in the wilderness. To the wise bird, every scarecrow is a dinner-gong, summoning him to an especially rich banquet, and he therefore keeps a sharp look-out for them, and rejoices whenever one appears.

Surely then the scarecrows which had so alarmed me were only pointing to richer blessings than any we had yet experienced. So the trip was fixed. My friend joined me at our mission station in Haifa, we filled the little car with our equipment and a huge supply of literature and off we started.

It was a wonderful privilege to go with Hope. She seemed to be quite unique in her real and sacrificial love for the people she worked among, and I was constantly put to shame. She was just about to leave the mission field under doctor's orders. Yet she insisted before leaving, on doing this difficult trip, and although often coughing and breathless and very weary she was quite undaunted, and willing to go on visiting and preaching long after I was feeling quite exhausted.

I shall never forget our first day together. We soon left the main road and began the long toilsome bumpy journeys which were all we could expect for the next few days. We took a wrong turning and lost our way quite early on in the proceedings, and unknown to ourselves crossed over into Transjordan instead of remaining on the Tiberias-Beisan track. We seemed to bump along the most awful track hour after hour, without seeing any kind of human habitation, or any creature to direct us on our way.

Inwardly I found this quite agonising, and pictured a hundred times over what we might expect if the car broke down in that remote desolation, and night should descend upon us, peopled with jackals, hyenas and wild tribesmen. We lurched forward in bottom gear, my mind wholly earthbound, both ears cocked for suspicious engine noises or the hiss or air escaping from the tires.

Hope sat beside me, quite evidently up in the heavenly places, her face radiant with pleasure, while she sang snatches of hymn tunes, and gave little ejaculations of delight at the beauty of the scenery. As far as she was concerned, the possibility of engine trouble or broken springs was non-existent, and I felt very earthly and wretched as I sat beside her, my heart thumping with apprehension. I knew that the Lord had promised that no harm should come to us, and I loathed and despised my own lack of faith. But the fact remained that while Hope was thoroughly enjoying the trip, the hours passed for me in misery.

However, towards the late afternoon, we suddenly emerged on to a better track and to our amazement arrived at the Jisr Majami Bridge and a custom house, where officials asked what we were doing in Transjordan without visas and permits. And there we had to wait while they rang up the police station in Beisan for permission to allow us to re-enter Palestine! This all being satisfactorily arranged, we drove on, and a little later we approached one of the settlements.

As soon as we drove into the gate, a crowd collected, very outspokenly astonished at receiving an unarmed and unescorted car in that out of the way spot, and doubly horrified when the visitors proved to be two solitary women. They gathered round expressing concern and amazement, and Hope explained that we were missionaries, and had brought them literature and Bibles, which we thought they might be glad to receive.

I had climbed stiffly out of the car, and stood a little on the outskirts of the group collected round Hope. The Maskir or leader of the settlement began to rebuke us. He asked if we knew that we were doing a mad and dangerous thing, driving about alone in that area? Did we not know that cars were frequently fired upon and that no one travelled without an escort? For two women to behave in this way was culpable presumption.

Hope replied that we had come because we believed that God had sent us, and we trusted in His protection and did not need an armed escort.

The leader replied firmly "And supposing you had been killed? What right have you to throw away your own life?"

I shall never forget watching the scene, and the expression on Hope's face as she looked round on the circle of astonished men. She answered in a clear, happy voice:

"But what does it matter if I lose my life as long as you have the opportunity to receive the Word of God, and hear about His gift of eternal life? I am very ready to die in order to bring it to you. We only come to you because we believe with all our hearts that this message is of eternal value to you, and of fearful importance. What happens to our mortal bodies is of no consequence whatsoever in comparison with the eternal truth we seek to tell you about. I tell you again I am ready to die in order to bring it to you."

There was nothing false or exaggerated in her statement, and it carried a tremendous weight of conviction. They knew as she spoke, that she meant it. She stood there, flushed with fever, her face radiant, all the tiredness and weakness of her body forgotten, as she spoke to them and offered the books she had brought.

I knew that I could not honestly echo her statement. I could not possibly begin to assure these lonely settlers that I cared enough about their souls to be ready to die in order to bring them the good news. I knew that nothing but a clear promise from the Lord that no harm should come to us had made we willing to start out on the trip. But Hope could say it truly, and her words carried the fullest conviction. The settlers felt it and responded. I envied her. She stood there, a very sick woman, unconscious of anything but the joy of being able to give her last message to these people. If she could but convey to them the word of life, she was supremely satisfied.

No wonder they crowded round and listened. I stood watching and praying, and wondering if I myself would ever feel the Wayfarer's real love for the people I was called to work amongst, as Hope felt it.

As evening drew on, and it was time to leave, the settlers followed us to the gate and stood watching our departure. We heard then a remark we were to hear many times in the future: "I wish I had real faith like yours, it must be very satisfying."

When we left we had only a few miles to go in order to reach the little Arab town of Beisan where two missionary ladies lived, and we arrived at their house about sunset. We were not expected, our letter having miscarried. But we received a wonderful welcome. It was a three-roomed cottage with a wide pillared verandah, and outside kitchen, with a fourth room standing alone in the garden, which was the prayer room and in which the little group of Christians met for their services. This room now became the guest chamber. Two beds were hurriedly pushed into it, and we were glad to lie down and rest awhile before the evening meal.

This little Christian home stood in a sheltered garden. There were a few young olive trees in it, and some pomegranates, then in blossom, their lovely red flowers glowing beautifully against the cloudless blue sky.

A brawling stream rushed by at the foot of the garden, and numbers of large kingfishers darted about like living sapphire gems. To me no bird is so beautiful as a kingfisher, and now I learnt for the first time that they sing too, a clear, long trill which filled all the garden, and made me think of Bunyan's birds, "With the melodious notes" which sang around the Palace Beautiful and also down in the Valley of Humiliation. Indeed the whole spot seemed so indescribably peaceful, and so full of a sort of radiant tranquility, that it must be one of "The King's Country Houses" where He loved to dwell. And those who lived there gave us the same kind of welcome He would give.

I lay in bed that night in the little prayer room, and listened to the leaves of the giant fig tree outside one of the windows, tapping on the glass, and through them caught the gleam of star shine. The whole night seemed full of the sound of running water, as the little torrent rushed past the garden, and ran joyfully down to join the distant river in the valley below, singing over and over again the song of all running water, that the lower one goes, the happier and fuller life becomes.

Next day Hope and I visited other settlements in the neighborhood, again over lonely and rough tracks, and again we met with the same remonstrances that we were mad and foolhardy to travel about alone, and again Hope explained that she was leaving the country and the doctor had said it was not likely that she would ever be able to return, and that she had longed to visit them and bring them the glad news of the living Saviour before she went away. The people were visibly impressed, and in one place, after the mid-day meal, she was allowed to address a few words to the whole assembled group.

As for the literature, we could not satisfy all the requests as received. We felt we must keep a reserve for the places still to be visited, and yet we could not bear to refuse anyone. None of our past visits had prepared me for such openings, and it soon became obvious that our supplies of literature were quite indadequate to meet the demand.

It is true there were often arguments, and objections were raised to our message, but only in a serious and interested spirit. Hope seemed to lose all sense of her bodily weakness and tiredness, and as long as there was anybody to listen she would go on witnessing. On every occasion on this trip I was forced to break up the talks and drag her away, when I felt that the time had come when we must leave if we were to get home by nightfall. When we did get back to the mission house, the reaction would set in, and she would cough for hours in the night, but always rose happy, cheerful and ready for the visits next morning.

After a few days we left our new friends and their happy little home in Beisan, and decided that for the following two nights we must try and sleep in one of the settlements in order to be able to reach the other more distant ones. I found to my shame and sorrow that I dreaded this prospect unspeakably. I could not bear to stay in these places with their bare huts, endless flies and above all the tiring crowds and complete lack of any privacy.

Also the atmosphere of these non-Christian places used to oppress me very much, and after a few hours in one of them it was always like throwing off a blanket of oppression when we got away. However, I knew it must be done and I prayed for grace, and envied Hope more than ever, for she looked forward to staying among the people, and hoped for still better opportunites to talk to them after the day's work was over.

In almost all these places we had the extraordinary experience of being mobbed by crowds eager for our literature, and especially for copies of the Scriptures, and on this particular day we had finally to struggle into the car and lock ourselves in with all the windows closed, to escape the crowds clamouring for books. It must be remembered in connection with this fact however, that in those days the settlers were terribly cut off from intercourse with others, and also that there was a real shortage of reading matter for them.

By mid-day we had given away every Bible and Testament that we had with us, even though the mission had already despatched us further supplies in answer to an S.O.S. call. We drove away at last and considered what we should do. We had no more literature, and yet two or three more places in the district remained unreached.

With a guilty sigh of relief I suggested to Hope that if she did not mind sleeping in a settlement that night as planned, I would hurry off in the car and get to our mission station by night, and replenish our stores and return to her the following afternoon. Hope gladly agreed to this suggestion. She had no objection at all to remaining on alone, and was glad that I was the one who would have the long drive and not herself, whereas I was guiltily rejoicing that by this plan I should be able once more to sleep at a comfortable mission station, and avoid one night at least in a settlement.

So we parted, and I drove off alone towards civilisation and comfort, and Hope remained behind. I reached our mission station about supper time and was able to give a glowing report on the wide open doors at every place we had been to. The Sisters of course were thrilled to hear about it, and so was the head of our mission, who was always most faithful in encouragement and prayer.

Early the next morning I crammed the car full of literature and started off again, and rejoined Hope in the afternoon. She had been happily employed in speaking with individuals in the settlement, and I found that she had been given a tiny room which she and one other woman had shared together. For this second night the other woman kindly gave up her place to me and went elsewhere, so that Hope and I had the unexpected privacy of a room to ourselves. However, there was only one hard lumpy bed in the room, and another lumpy mattress had been laid on the floor.

I looked at these preparations for the night's rest with a sinking heart. The bed looked horrible enough but that thin lumpy thing on the floor looked impossible. It was fearfully hot and I was very tired. And so was Hope. And Hope had endured the place for two whole days and a night, and I had slept comfortably in my own room the night before.

Hope was feverish and weak. Obviously, the bed must be for her, and in that case, just as obviously, those lumps on the floor must be for me. But somehow I simply could not open my mouth and say casually and unconcerned, "Hop into bed Hope, I want the mattress." The words just stuck in my throat. And Hope, still happily talking over the happenings of the day, undressed, and as a simple matter of course, and as though no other idea had ever entered her head, lay down on the floor.

I felt almost sick with shame, but only managed the feeblest expostulation: "Oh, Hope, hadn't you better have the bed? Do you think you will be able to sleep like that?"

And her cheery, surprised reply "Why of course, Grace. I wouldn't think of taking the bed. I am accustomed to sleeping on the floor and you are not."

It was quite one of the worst memories I have. My cheeks still burn as I recall her stretching herself out on the thin little mattress on the floor, where she lay coughing and gasping for some time, and myself miserable and wretched, but doggedly selfish, lying on the bed.

Only a few months ago when Hope and I met again after a long absence, we were recalling that trip and rejoicing together over the memories then eight or nine years old. And I suddenly burst out, hot and shame-faced, "But there is one memory of that time which I simply hate to recall, the way I let you sleep on the floor and kept the bed for myself. What a despicable, selfish beast I was!"

And Hope turned her kind, affectionate look upon me and said, incredulously, "I don't believe you ever did such a thing Grace. I certainly don't remember it. I believe its just your invention."

That is one of the very loveliest outcomes of the village work, the wonderful friends it has given me and the influence they have had on my life. Hope never guessed for a moment what companionship with her in that work had meant to me personally, nor the vision I got through her, at that time, of a love which is truly unconscious of self.

The next day we reached the last settlement, and late that evening returned to the home town. From start to finish nothing had gone wrong with the car and we had not even had a puncture.

Seven or eight months had passed since beginning the village work, and what a lot of ground had already been covered. And by this time the work had become a joyous obsession. We would go on till all the Jewish settlements in the country had been visited, and then we would start again.

The black boundary line which I had made around our own district had become meaningless. But still not a glimmer of the real plan ahead had dawned. I was full of praise and joy that the promise had been so gloriously fulfilled about the open door which no man could shut. It was wonderful to feel that I was launched out into itinerant evangelistic work at last, and that God had so gloriously provided fellow helpers.

A few days later Hope sailed for home. I went down to the harbour with her when the time came for her to embark. She was very reserved and she had said all her farewells already, and I was the only one seeing her off. Neither of us knew whether she would be able to return or not. It was dark, and we stood together almost wordlessly on the quay, unable to find any way of expressing our feelings. Then she went alone on the gangway, and at the top turned and waved, before disappearing into the ship.

As I watched her go I felt a sense of the most painful loss. She, more than anyone I knew, had made me feel the littleness and selfishness of my own heart, and had shamed away all my smug thoughts about my own missionary zeal. We were poles apart in zeal and love. It was not just words with her, she had meant it quite literally when she had said, "I would be glad to die if I could bring you the gift of life." As I turned back alone into the crowded city, I prayed desperately and longingly, that the Great Shepherd Himself would teach me some time, and by some means, to find and follow the same path of love.

6
TRUE YOKE—FELLOW

"Ye shall go out with joy, and be led forth with peace" (Is. 55:12).

By this time Peace had married and Hope had left the country. As I thought and prayed about the many unvisited districts and the problem of how to reach them, I felt more and more convinced that what was really needed in order to reach the villages in districts where there were no missionaries at all, was for a full time fellow worker. And just about the time that Hope left, I received a letter from the missionary who had visited me on her way home to England the year before, and to whom I had spoken about the call to this evangelistic work.

She wrote to say that her year's furlough was drawing to an end, and she hoped to return in the autumn. During the time she had been at home the thought of the settlements had been a burden on her mind. She had been thrilled to hear about the work which had been started, and it had come to her very clearly that it was God's plan, having called us both to the same kind of work, that we should unite, and she would like to come and join me in the autumn, and we would make a full-time job of visiting these places.

This letter was a tremendous thrill. Here was another person who had received an identical call with my own, at just about the same time, and was free and willing to launch out with me on the task. We both had the same aims and the same longing to reach the unreached places.

We had trained at the same Bible college and were like-minded in belief, and as far as we could judge, in method. But—and it was a very big but—tempera-mentally we were very unlike, and would probably find it very difficult to work together. This feeling was emphasised when we saw how our mutual friends reacted to the idea of our joining forces. One and all exclaimed, "Oh you and Faith will never fit in together. I am afraid that you will both find that you are unsuited to each other."

Fortun-ately both Faith and I were fully alive to this fact and admitted it honestly to each other as soon as we met. We talked it over quite openly and seriously and discussed the difficulties, and yet we both felt more and more assured that God had brought us together and we must claim His power and the real unity which only He could give.

As we compared notes as to how He had called both of us, and put the burden of the unreached places on our hearts at the same time, it became more and more evident that we must be meant to unite in the work, if only we could be kept from clashing.

As we frankly discussed this likelihood together, both of us overjoyed at the thought of being called to such work, and yet terribly conscious of not really liking each other very much, Faith said earnestly, "Grace, it seems so clear that God has called us both and brought us together, I think we really must claim His power to enable us to work together, however unlikely our friends feel that it will be."

And I said, "Faith if you are willing to make the attempt, I shall be only too thankful to do so too."

I am purposely entering into details on this subject, because the matter of adjusting oneself to working harmoniously with temperamentally uncongenial fellow workers is one of the greatest problems on the mission field, and the whole future of the work we had been called to, hung on whether our Lord could make us able to pull together or not, for certainly we were a very unlikely pair.

The chief causes of possible friction were the following:

Faith was the senior, both in age and in length of time on the mission field, and yet she had been in England ever since this work started, and I already had a year's experience. Who then was to take the lead?

She, like Hope, was a real spartan, and ready to face any hardship and discomfort, indeed the more discomfort the better. To live as much as possible like the people we visited was her aim, and to her way of thinking a messenger of the Lord would, as a matter of course, go on until they dropped from weariness, and then still further if necessary. All one's time and strength should be poured out in glad service for the Lord.

I on the other hand, was a definite lover of ease, and I shrank from discomfort of any kind. Moreover I felt it foolish and unnecessary to work until one dropped, and held the view that we should keep ourselves as fit as possible for the Lord's work, and that one simply could not do good work if one was dead tired, quite unnecessarily. The Lord we serve is not a taskmaster, always goading us on to tasks we felt too tired or ill to do.

We were well aware, therefore, from the very beginning, that we would be unlikely to agree on the number of hours to be spent visiting, and that I would be for turning home long before she thought it necessary.

Again, Faith was very methodical in all her planning and thinking. Her method would be to plan out with scrupulous care, all the villages most easily reached at the same time or from the same centre, and to go doggedly on until each place could be crossed off, and never to turn back until all had been reached. Method and careful planning were her strong points.

I on the other hand, felt very bound and hampered by fixed plans, and my method was to spread the map out and wait in silent prayer for the Lord to lay on our minds and hearts the place He would have us try and reach, and which, we could trust, He would have been specially preparing for our coming.

In this way, if, when we started out we found the way temporarily blocked, or apparently impassable, Faith's instinct was to press on at any cost, and never turn back. My instinct was to stop at the block and wait on the Lord to see if this was His indication that we were to go to some other village, and return to the one originally planned at a later date. Sometimes we had found that when obliged to turn back, some other door had been opened for us, and the initial difficulty had been all part of God's guidance.

There were other very real divergencies of opinion and temperament. And added to this was the fact, well known to both of us, that we both loved to lead and take the initiative. No wonder our friends looked askance at the idea of our working together.

It was Faith, undoubtedly, who made the plan possible. She said from the very beginning, "As you have been doing this work for a year Grace, and I have had no experience, you lead and I will back you up." It cost her still more to add, "And when you are really tired it is for you to say when we turn back."

We decided that we would put aside one whole morning each week for prayer and for seeking the Lord's guidance and strength, and for claiming, before setting out on our visits, an open door and victory in each place we planned to go to.

This we did. We set aside

every Saturday morning for the special work of prayer and preparation. And without doubt, it was this habit of spending Saturday morning together in the company of our Lord, that worked the miracle and overcame our temperamental differences, and welded us together in the closest possible friendship. I suggest this method as easily the best and surest way of reaching real harmony and unity in service.

We pored over the map together, and talked over routes, and we frankly discussed together our methods, the things that jarred and the things we thought had hindered or helped. And when we had thoroughly covered the whole ground, consciously remembering all the time that we were speaking, that our Lord was present and hearing every word, and trusting Him to control and direct our planning we then settled down to prayer and communion with Him.

We both quickly recognized the value of beginning with a time of silent waiting on the Lord. In this silence we both came to Him and offered ourselves to Him, and became completely absorbed in His presence, asking for our minds and thoughts to be cleansed, and that we might be brought to real unity in understanding His will.

Generally this silent communion with the Lord lasted about half-an-hour. Sometimes we were so absorbed in His presence that words would not come at all, and whole hours passed in silence. There is nothing, in such times of silent communion, of making the mind a blank and waiting for ideas to come as it were out of the blue. But rather, communion of this kind demands that every part of the mind and will be actively and joyfully handed over to the Lord for Him to use.

There is nothing passive about it, but the most active co-operation possible, and though at first one may feel desperately dull and heavy, and the thought of prayer and vital communion, almost impossible, the Holy Spirit invariably comes to quicken and empower, so that by the end of those mornings of prayer, we had not only listened to the Lord, and been led to victories of faith, but our minds and bodies had also undergone a wonderful renewal of strength and refreshment.

At the end of this silent time we generally found that we had been led to complete unity on the points we had differed about, or not been sure of. Then we prayed about every matter that the Lord brought into our minds in connection with the work. We prayed for individuals. We claimed a victory against the powers of evil who would try and thwart the next visits. We claimed open doors, and the liberation of those who wanted to get free, and we confessed our failures and asked for the needed wisdom and understanding in connection with any problem.

And from the very beginning of this inauguration of a weekly prayer day, for it generally continued well into the afternoon, we found a real love for one another growing in our hearts, and a most amazingly joyful fellowship developing.

We tried to be very frank with one another, and to talk

over personal difficulties if it seemed necessary, but not until we had had our time of silent communion with the Lord first, and been brought so close to Him, that we could speak over these things with real love and gentleness. That, I think, is one very important point in achieving victory and harmony. It is never well to speak of personal — faults or irritating matters, unless there has first been a time of coming to the Lord together in united silence, humility and faith.

My own experience has been that as long as the irritating matter is able to haunt one's thoughts during that time of silent worship, and one is unable to get free of it, but goes over the point again and again, one can be sure that the matter has not been fully yielded to the Lord, and one is not in a prepared frame of mind to mention it without aggravating the situation. It is better to keep silent on the matter altogether under those circumstances, and wait till the Lord has brought one to the place of being able to put it on one side, and has set one at liberty to think and pray for other needs.

And from the very first we had happy times together as we went from house to house. Undoubtedly there is nothing better for developing close friendship and understanding than going out on such work and challenging together the powers of darkness. The fact that we both felt so helpless and so utterly cast upon the Lord, drew us very close to each other. Always we prayed together outside the village before going in, and always on the way home after the work was over, we experienced the same wonderful joy.

Also we became much more accustomed to visiting the communal type of settlement which Peace and I found so hard to tackle at the beginning. We aimed, whenever possible, to reach these places about mid-day, and we would go straight to the big dining-room and announce as soon as we entered, that we were missionaries and had brought literature with us. We often sat down at different tables and made a point of letting everybody sitting at the table know who we were, and why we had come.

This never got any easier, but it was quite successful, and often scores of people would gather round while we still sat at the table, and begin discussing the matter with us, and asking for literature, and of course trying to argue with us. We found a real hunger for reading matter in these places. Often of course the arguments and objections raised would be quite heated, but we tried to confine ourselves to stating simply the reason for our visit and our own personal experience of the joy and power which comes from personal contact with Christ.

7
PLACING
THE DYNAMITE

"I am not ashamed of the gospel of Christ, for it is the power (the dynamite) of God unto salvation to everyone that believeth" (Rom. 1:16).

It was not until several years had passed that we began to hear of any results from all this visiting; but there were real results developing even then, and fruit we were to rejoice over with awed amazement later on.

One particular hot unpleasant day, as we toiled round from house to house in a settlement, we had several good talks, and one or two rather difficult receptions. That was all we knew for a long time. Then, one day four or five years later, we heard more of what happened after we had left. One woman who came to the door in answer to our knock was very annoyed to find that we were missionaries. But she softened a little when she noticed that we both looked very hot and tired, and began asking herself why two women should bother to go round from house to house on such a hot day.

It seemed then that we asked her if she would be kind enough to give us a drink of water, and she answered "Oh, yes of course, even if you are missionaries, I will give you a cup of water. Come inside and I will bring it." Then we spoke to her for a while inside the house, but she was not very impressed apparently by anything that we said, but only by the fact that we seemed to think it worth while to do such work on such a hot day.

When we left we presented her with a Bible. She picked it up as soon as we had left, and turned with curiosity to the New Testament which she had never in her life read before. The first words her eye fell upon were, "Whosoever shall give you a cup of water to drink in my name shall in no wise lose his reward. He that receiveth you, receiveth Me" (Matt. 10:42, 40).

She was absolutely staggered. She said to herself, "Can it really be true that in giving a glass of water to these two Christian women, I have done it to the One I have always been taught to believe was an imposter and blasphemer?"

She read eagerly on, and then turned back to the beginning of the New Testament she began reading there. Day after day she read on until she had read the whole New Testament from beginning to end, and then she read it through a second time. By that time, she said, she was fully convinced that the Book was true, that Jesus was the promised Messiah and the Son of God. She began talking to her neighbors, and reading to them, until several of them met every week in her house to study the New Testament.

She made several trips into the town to the Bible shop in order to buy Testaments for this little group. She stated that they all believed, though they were afraid to confess it openly because their husbands would be angry. And she ended by saying to our friend in the Bible shop, "I felt I must tell you about this, so that you can tell those two ladies their work has not been in vain, and to encourage them to go on with it."

But often the work was very difficult. On one occasion a woman came to the door, a very orthodox Jewess. As soon as she learned who we were and heard the name of the Lord Jesus mentioned, she burst into a torrent of abuse, spitting continually every time she or we mentioned the precious name of the Saviour. "May His name be blotted out" she shouted, and spat again. "An imposter! A blasphemer! May His memory be forgotten."

It seemed impossible for us to accomplish anything at her house, or even to leave literature, for she spat again at sight of a proffered gospel and tried to snatch it from us and tear it up. As we stood patiently listening to her abuse and hoping a moment's opportunity might arise for us to drop a seed thought, I noticed that her two grown-up daughters, who had been standing silently behind her, were looking wistfully at me, and I left Faith to continue listening to the mother, and turned quietly towards them. One daughter put her finger on her lips and then motioned me closer.

The woman was still furiously addressing Faith and did not notice us, and the elder of the daughters leant towards me and whispered quickly, "Give me one of those books. My sister and I would like to read it. We will hide it." I quickly slipped a New Testament into her hand, and she hid it under her apron and turned away, and stood quietly by her sister while her mother finished her harangue. She mentioned the Saviour's name once more, spat again, and announced that she had finished with us. We turned away feeling that it was no use to try and say more at that juncture, and yet praying earnestly that God would bless and use the Testament which so unexpectedly had found its way into that closed house.

Another time as we were visiting a village, and going from door to door, we had several rather difficult receptions, and we came finally to a little house, where it so happened that a young man was working in the garden. As soon as he heard that we were offering Christian literature, he became very angry, and pronounced a curse upon the name of the Christian Saviour. We asked him if he had ever read the gospel for himself, and when he replied vehemently that such a blasphemous record should never be opened or read by himself, we answered that it seemed unjust to judge and condemn the teaching of the Lord Jesus without first studying it for himself, or at least first reading it through.

We held out a little Testament as we spoke. For a moment it looked as though he would spit on it. His eyes blazed. But to our surprise he controlled himself and asked after a moment, "Is that book the account of your Saviour?"

We said "Yes."

"Then give it to me," he said. We handed it over rather hesitatingly. He turned at once to the house, and a moment or two later reappeared holding a long handled shovel on which were burning coals, and the little Testament already in flames, lying on the top. He held it out in front of us while it burnt, and we stood silently watching the Book which might have brought him the message of life, flaming and crackling and falling into ashes.

A remarkable thing happened as we watched. It seemed as though the Lord Himself actually stood with us, watching with patient sorrow and yet with steady determination, while the man's angry face brooded over the fiery fragments, until with a final curse he tossed the charred remains into the garbage bin. "There goes the record of your Jesus," he flung at us through clenched teeth. A great flood of love and sorrow seemed to break over by heart. A love and pain unlike anything I had felt before.

At that moment it seemed that no cost would be too great if this man could find the Saviour. But it seemed that there was nothing that we could do. "I hate Him!" exclaimed the man turning to us again, "I hate Him."

"Yes," I said, "I see that you hate Him. But I would do almost anything if I could help you understand that though you hate Him so much, He loves you with an everlasting love. And this one thing we will tell you before we leave. He will go on loving you and seeking to make you realize His love, as long as you live.

"You have burnt the book which would have brought you the message of His love, but the Saviour Himself you cannot destroy, nor His love even for those who reject Him. He came to you today and you would not listen. But, believe me, He will come again and again with the most patient and determined love, and will go on pleading with you."

So we turned away, and went and knelt together in a quiet place outside the village, and asked that the charred, and yet not wholly burnt Testament, lying on the garbage heap, might still carry its message.

So several months passed by.

It was a great blow to me, when in the middle of this happy and exciting work, I was obliged to go to the hospital for some weeks and leave Faith to carry on the work with the help of different friends who volunteered to go out with her.

And all unknown to us the moment was approaching for a new challenge of faith, and a call to widen and enlarge the work we were engaged in, in a manner neither of us had ever dreamt about.

8
THE WAYFARER'S OTHER SHEEP

"Other sheep I have, which are not of this fold, them also I must bring and they shall hear My voice" (John 10:16).

It was during my first week in the mission hospital at Nazareth lying quietly in bed, and praying that the Lord would make use of the time thus spent, and would teach me more of His will and plan, that I began to feel a growing sense that there was some special matter that He wanted to speak to me about, though I had no idea what it was.

This strange, inner certainty grew, and seemed to press more and more strongly on my mind, so that I found myself constantly led to pray, "Lord, show me what it is that Thou dost want me to understand."

One morning early, as I was trying to keep the daily quiet time with the Lord, He turned me to a verse which had lingered in my memory from Bible college days, "Come with Me, and look from the top" (Cant. 4:8). Suggesting our great need before ever beginning to pray, of ascending the mountain with the Lord, so as to be able to look at things from His view point and not from our low, limited, earthly one. It seemed to me that morning in my memory from Bible college days: "Come with Me, and look from the top. I have something to show you that you have never properly noticed before."

I earnestly committed myself to Him and asked that I might indeed be able to go up to the mountain top with Him, and get a clear vision of what it was He wanted to show me. Then it seemed to me that in spirit I was standing with Him on a mountain top, looking out over the whole land spread out before us, the mountains and plains and valleys which during the past two years of continual travel, we were coming to know so well. And I thought He said to me, "Grace, what do you see?"

And in my mind's eye, as I looked out over the land spread out before me like the map which Faith and I so continually studied, I saw all the Jewish settlements we had visited during those two years, carrying to them the word of life and offering it to as many as possible, and I thought I saw green trails to each of those places, as though a tiny rivulet of water had trickled to them. I looked away southward to the places I knew Faith and her helpers were even then trying to reach, to the hundred or more settlements where as yet no channel for the water of life had been cut. And I began to pray that very soon the water might begin to flow to them too.

By this time I knew the map

of Palestine by heart as far as these settlements were concerned. I knew how many there were in every district and the tracks by which to reach each one. And the sight of the green trails marking those tracks and reminding me that the Word of God had been carried to all those places, greatly rejoiced my heart.

But even as I looked, a heavy, almost intolerable burden, began to press upon me, a certainty that the Lord wanted to show me something else, and although I still did not know what it was, I knew I shrank from being shown.

Then He seemed to say, "Look again, Grace. Not just at the villages with the green trails. What else do you see?"

Very wretchedly I raised my eyes and looked again. And as I stared out over the land spread out before us, I saw what He wanted me to see. Not just a few hundred Jewish settlements where the people spoke Hebrew, but on all the hills, and in every valley and scattered over the plains, hundred and hundreds of mud villages became visible, dirty, primitive, miserable places, where the people spoke a language I had never learnt, and practised another religion, that of Islam.

And as I looked out over the land, I saw out in the deserts, and in the hidden valleys between the mountains, unnumbered tents belonging to wandering tribes who had no settled villages. And as I stared and stared, sick at heart, I heard my Lord say, "Why do you never pray for all those places, Grace? Who is carrying My message to them? Is the water of life not meant for all these villages too?"

I remember how fiercely I answered because I knew now what it was He was going to say, and I was afraid to hear it. So I exclaimed, "Lord the task you have given us is already taking all our time and strength. And here I am lying in the hospital, not strong enough to finish even the first round to the villages You called us to.

"What concern of mine are all those hundreds of other places? I do not know Arabic. I have not studied their religion. You told us to claim that every Jewish settlement should be reached. There are only a few hundred of them. But there are many hundreds of these other places. Why do you speak to me about them? What concern are they of mine? We have claimed the ones you told us to, and Faith is carrying on the work. Is not that enough?"

And He said, "Now I want you to claim every place in the land, every single village, and every single encampment. The water of life must be taken to them all. You ask what concern they are of yours? They are all My concern. I want to visit every place. Are you ready to go with Me?"

I did not know how to answer. I lay there and remembered how, as we travelled along the roads to the settlements, I had begun noticing all the other countless Arab villages we passed on the way, houses and walls all built of dried mud, and how in each district, as we met the different missionaries, I had begun enquiring as to who was visiting these places. Over and over again the answer had been, "No one. We are too understaffed here." Or, "We have no car." Or, "The Bible woman is too old now to get about." Or, "We have lost our evangelist."

I remember the growing sense of being vaguely disturbed, which always came over me as I listened to these replies. It was sad the missions could not send out evangelists, but it was not our concern.

And then I suddenly remembered sitting on a hillside at Nazareth one afternoon, and looking out towards one of the settlements Faith and I were wanting to visit. And as I prayed for the people there, I noticed four or five other mud villages within sight of the one place we were aiming to go to. Perhaps no one was praying for these other villages, that the word of life might be carried to the illiterate, ignorant people living in them. And I remembered the distinct way in which I had seemed to hear the Lord say, "Other sheep I have, them also I must bring." And I realized that He had been preparing me for many weeks, for the thing He was saying to me that morning.

He wanted every village visited. The water of life must be carried to all. But why was He speaking to me?

I lay there in a hospital bed, and my friends were saying I was not strong enough for the work we had already undertaken. In a few weeks I was due to start for England again. Mentally I went over the little group of those interested in the work. Hope was out of the country. Another had a strained heart. Peace was married. I myself was in the hospital. Apparently only Faith was still fit and free. And we had only one tiny baby Austin car between us. And not one of us who had been doing this visiting work, knew one word of the Arabic language spoken in these many hundred mud villages, and in the encampments. What could the Lord mean? I turned to Him in desperation:

"Tell me, and make me able and willing to understand what it is You want me to understand this morning."

And He said, "I want you and the others to claim that every single place in the whole land will be reached with the word of life. I want you to begin making the need known. I want you to start prayer centres in every district, where My people will pray that every single place in that district will be visited. And as a start must be made by someone, I want you to make that start. You cannot preach yourself through lack of Arabic. But you can drive someone who can preach. I want you to be My chauffeur. Are you willing?"

How wonderful it would be to be able to accept joyfully, and with perfect willingness from the very beginning, whatever the Lord asks of us. I could not at that moment accept joyfully, but He did help me to say I was willing, and that I trusted Him to make me do it gladly when the time came. But the actual feeling just then was one of overwhelming dread and dismay. Moreover, when the quiet time was finished, and I came down from the mountain top, the whole thing began to look so utterly impossible and crazy that I thought I must be mad.

The temptation constantly came, to think that I had imagined the whole thing, and had quite misunderstood the Lord. I had been called to mission work among the Jews and had joined a missionary society which worked among those people alone. I had given all my time to them and to the study of their language. I did not know one word of Arabic. Then was I not being tempted to turn away from my real task? Wasn't it just a phase of restlessness? And wasn't I becoming a rolling stone, unable to carry on steadily with one particular task?

Then Faith came to visit me, and I shared with her the amazing call, which I felt I must persist in believing I had received. Naturally she was somewhat taken aback, especially as we had only one car between us, and I spoke of launching out to every village in the country, and we had still not finished reaching all the settlements she and I had been called to together.

But it was characteristic of Faith, that after we had talked the matter over, and had prayed about it, she should enter into it with full faith and support. Of course all the Arab villages must hear as well! Why hadn't we thought of it before? We must ask God to give us another car, and meanwhile she would keep and use the one we had, while I was in England. And for the few weeks which remained before I left, I would use it one day a week for making a start to the new villages. That is, if I was strong enough to make a start at all, and could find someone with knowledge of the language, free, and ready to go with me.

My complete ignorance, due to lack of interest, of any work among the Moslem population made it seem almost impossible to know how to start. I had mixed almost entirely with missionaries engaged in work among the Jews and I scarcely knew any others. And who among them would want to launch out into this new work with a person who had never been interested enough to learn a word of the necessary language, nor to study the religious beliefs of the people?

Well, at any rate, as the Lord had said, I could offer myself as chauffeur, and I must trust Him to lead me to the ones He must have prepared to do the preaching.

9
LAUNCHING OUT INTO THE DEEP

"God hath chosen the foolish things of the world to confound the wise, and God hath chosen the weak things of the world, to confound the things which are mighty" (I Cor. 1:27).

When I left the hospital and returned to Haifa, our mission town, where I had been living alone in the Jewish quarter, our own doctor came to visit me. I felt I must burn my boats behind me, and so I told him of the new call. I felt sure he would laugh at the very idea, and say I had better at least put it off until I returned from furlough in England. He would point out all the reasons why it was absurd and impossible. Instead, he listened quietly and then said:

"Well, you will just have time to make a start before you leave for England, and then it will be easier for you to launch out steadily on your return."

I was astounded, and even a little indignant. I said with feeble reproach: "I don't feel fit or strong enough to start on such a tremendous undertaking. And I keep wondering if I have misunderstood the Lord."

But he would not give me one scrap of sympathy, nor one tiny excuse to doubt. He said firmly: "It turned out that you had heard Him aright when He first called you to visit the Jewish settlements. Why doubt Him this time? All those Moslem villages ought to hear the gospel. Someone must make a start, and if He has called you, the sooner you start the better. It gets more difficult to obey if one puts it off."

I made one last effort to escape. "But I don't know a single person who would be free and ready to go with me."

And then he told me of a missionary who had been living for many years in a lonely village among the people, and who had recently come to stay in our town, with her Bible woman. He suggested that I should call on them and see if they were willing to go out with me.

So as soon as possible I called upon Miss Piety. Her Bible woman, Mother of Hope, was with her. When I spoke to them of the burden on my heart for all the Moslem villages, their faces lit up with real joy, and Miss Piety told me that twenty years ago it had been her work to itinerate in the villages, preaching the gospel. But for many years she had been obliged to give up the itinerant work. She longed to re-visit some of the villages, and agreed to go with me, although it seemed a particularly dangerous and ridiculous time to start itinerating, as the Arab-Jewish disturbances were in full swing, and dangerous terrorist bands were lurking in the mountains and raiding the villages for supplies. But as God had given the call, she was willing to try.

The Bible woman was going home for a holiday, but she herself would go out with me one day that same week. If God opened the way for us, and set His seal on our going out, she and the Mother of Hope would visit with me each week until I went home.

I was almost overwhelmed with joy and awe. I asked her what place she would like to visit first. She mentioned a big village about twenty miles away, which she had stayed in twenty years before, I looked it up on the map and found it was easily accessible, and we arranged to set forth together that very week.

It is impossible not to laugh now as I look back on my feelings when the day came to set out on the first visit. To me, the Moslems we were going to were all fierce, primitive creatures, continually stabbing one another, carrying on blood feuds, firing on foreigners, and holding up and robbing travellers. And the thought of venturing unarmed and alone into one of their lonely, wild villages, and trying to preach to them about a Saviour, for whom they felt only a fanatical contempt or even hate, seemed to me a frightfully dangerous undertaking.

Also I dreaded the squallor and the dirt, and the fact that Miss Piety firmly emphasised that we must eat and drink whatever was offered to us, or we should offend the people and make them feel that we were unwilling to be friendly.

And on top of everything it was an appallingly hot day, and I was still feeling weak and nervous, and quite unable in myself to face the ordeal of plunging for the first time into a primitive village where I would not understand a single word that was spoken. Miss Piety herself had not done such work for many years, and she too was feeling a little nervous, especially as she had always been accustomed to having a Bible woman with her, and this time she had no one but a speechless and inexperienced companion. Our friends too, were full of warnings and grave forbodings about road mines and terrorist gangs, and altogether our frame of mind when we set off, was far from enviable.

It was a good thing that we did not know at that stage, what we discovered after arrival at our destination, that the village we had chosen had just got itself into serious trouble for harbouring and supporting the leader of an Arab terrorist gang who had been raiding other villages for supplies. The gang had been allowed to store their arms in this village and the rebel chief made his headquarters there.

An armed force had been sent to clear the district of these rebels, the village had been entered, and the hidden arms were discovered, although the terrorists themselves escaped. As a punishment some of the leading men of the village had been carried off to prison, the house where the arms were found had been destroyed, and for two days no one had been allowed to leave or enter the village, the armed force making a cordon round the village and

10
WIDENING HORIZONS

"Who can have compassion on the ignorant, and on them that are out of the way" (Heb. 5:2).

Thus a start was made in great weakness and with much fear and trembling, to obey the call of the Wayfarer to go with Him to all the villages, and we were committed to the great adventure of trying to reach every place in the whole country.

It was at this time that the Lord spoke to us in a very special way through the story of the feeding of the more than five thousand hungry people with what seemed such hopelessly inadequate supplies, five loaves and two small fishes. For Faith and I were the only two people free for whole time itinerant work and we had five part-time helpers and what were we among so many? How could these multitudes of villages be reached by so few messengers who had only one small car between them?

And looking back on it now, and recalling our complete lack of experience, it seems extraordinary that God was able to make us believe that the thing was possible. But as we thought together of how He had made the five loaves and the two small fishes which were offered to Him, enough to meet and satisfy the need of so many thousands, so we were challenged and helped to believe and claim that He would use us to meet the need of all these unreached multitudes, and that He would make it possible for all of them to hear the word of life. All we needed to do was to offer ourselves to Him without reserve or doubt.

A week after the start had been made as already described, Miss Piety and her Bible woman and I, went to a second village, a much smaller and poorer place. Here we found that almost all the inhabitants, men and women alike, were out in the harvest field, and only a handful of sick or old women remained in the village. We were not therefore, taken to the public guest room, but a dirty tattered mat was spread on the ground outside one of the one-roomed mud huts, and here we sat, with four or five women in their long black peasant dresses, squatting before us.

The village was on a hill, and there was a wonderful view of sun-baked plain and distant snow-capped Hermon spread out before us. But this audience was very different from the one in the crowded room in the first village. These poor peasant women simply sat and stared at us with apathetic curiosity, and seemed so completely uninterested in the preaching, that at last Mother of Hope paused and asked if they did not want to listen.

I have never

forgotten the answer made by one of them, a young wife, perhaps sixteen years of age, with a tired, lifeless face and unhappy eyes. "Why do you come and try to talk to us about such things? Our men folk might understand, but we are only like the cows and sheep, and we know nothing about anything except the daily happenings of our lives. It is no good trying to teach us anything new."

We could do little more on that occasion than tell one or two Bible stories and use the Wordless Book with the four colours. But we left one gospel to be given, we hoped, to the head man, who was almost the only person in the village who could read.

In those earlier years, on almost every occasion when we had a gathering of Moslem women only, we experienced the same difficulty. It was almost impossible to gain their attention, or when gained, to hold it for more than five minutes. They had never gone to school, never learned to listen and concentrate, and though they would gather out of curiosity and stare at the strange women, and finger our clothes and lift our dresses to see if there was anything underneath, and even poke their fingers in our hair to see if it felt like their own, we were almost always in despair to know how to make them listen.

Even if they appeared to be listening, we would discover in the end, that they had really been staring at some portion of our clothes or some physical feature which had provoked special curiosity, and that not a word spoken had penetrated their minds.

It is true they would listen with interest to a graphically told story, provided it was short, but without any conception at all that it might have a personal application to themselves, and when we tried to apply the story to their own lives and needs, it would be like trying to make water stay on a duck's back. Even the Bible women with their fluent language, found it almost impossible to interest these poor peasant women, and they greatly preferred preaching to a room full of men.

As women were generally not allowed in the village guest room, if we wanted to preach to them, we usually waited till we had finished with the men, and then asked if we might be allowed to sit awhile with the women in their part of the house. Or else, after leaving the guest room, we would see a whole group of women squatting in a mud courtyard or in the dusty streets, and then we would go and squat down beside them for a few minutes, and tell a gospel story and try and speak to them about the Saviour. But it was always easier and better to try and do our preaching indoors.

There were too many interruptions outside. A horde of noisy children would collect; cattle would pass along the narrow lane, smothering us in clouds of dust, and forcing us to press ourselves against the mud walls; or a sudden gust of wind would fill our eyes and noses with dust and our hair with loose straw and chaff. And sometimes passers-by would gather and interrupt, or begin to argue, so that whenever possible we preferred to be inside. If the head man or some member of his family was at home, we felt it best to claim his hospitality, and wait for people to gather in their own accustomed meeting place, the village guest room.

We quickly found also that it was wisest to practise the same principle in these villages as in the very different settlements; that is to make it clear at once that we were missionaries, and that we had come to visit them because we felt we had an important message from God to give them, and we should be grateful if all who wanted to hear it, could be allowed to come to the guest room and listen. This very seldom failed to produce the result we wanted.

On the other hand, if we did not make this explanation at once, we were generally taken to be the wives of high government officials, or lady doctors, or important educational officials, and a feast would at once be prepared for us, and then it was difficult and embarrassing to explain that we had enoyed a welcome to which we were unentitled.

Even so, we were nearly always most courteously received and would be taken to the guest room. As long as there was at least one foreign lady in the party, this was quite correct, but women of the country going alone to the villages, would be considered as greatly lacking in propriety if they asked to be taken to the public guest room, which is always the jealously preserved meeting place for men alone.

Inside the guest room, mattresses would immediately be spread for us upon the floor and for about half-an-hour or so, while the coffee was being prepared, men would collect in ones and twos, and sit around the walls, conversing with·us. It was never wise to begin preaching until the coffee was made and offered, or else there would be a great interruption when it was ready, and once the preaching was interrupted, it was not easy to get started again.

So we used to utilise the waiting time by asking friendly questions about the village; the state of the crops; the general health of the inhabitants; whether the village had a school or not; and questions about the head man's family and the number of his children, etc. The more friendly the atmosphere which we could create in this way, the greater would be our opportunity later on for preaching to an attentive and interested audience. For in these villages, where none of the women, and only a very small minority of the men, could read and write, it was intensely important to gather as many as possible to listen to the message, and to create a favourable atmosphere so that those who came would be disposed to listen willingly.

In such places it was only possible to leave behind four or five gospels with the few who could read, and those who did not come to listen would be left untouched. Therefore, the preaching of the message was a tremendous responsibility.

There were plenty of amusing incidents also. In one very distant village, isolated from the rest of the world by an exceedingly bad track, we met a very old, almost toothless peasant woman, who on seeing strangers in such an out-of-the-way place, stopped to satisfy her curiosity as to the reason for our presence. She peered at me in a critical and considering manner, and evidently not recognising me as a foreigner, said something to the Bible woman which I did not catch, but which my friend translated to me with great glee:

"Is that your daughter you have brought with you from the town? I suppose you are looking for a husband for her? But she is a bit too old and ugly even for a village man."

11
JOURNEYING MERCIES

*"When thou goest, thy steps shall not be strait-
ened, and when thou runnest, thou shalt not
stumble" (Prov. 4:12).*

This was the promise the
Lord gave us when the time came for us to launch
out with whatever helpers He would provide for us,
in an effort to reach every place in the country.

By
this time many new friends had become interested
in the work, and one of them most kindly lent us a
second car, much larger and stronger than the baby
Austin. Soon, as we pressed on with our work in
different districts, other missions were ready to
allow their Bible women and evangelists to share
with us in the work, and we gradually developed
into a small, but very happy and enthusiastic band
of village preachers. Indeed, God's plan for reaching every place, though it had looked so impossible
at first, unfolded itself before us gradually but
quite plainly, like an opening flower.

It was very
simple. In every district where there were already

missionaries interested in the work we would make our headquarters with them, and go out with their Bible women, nurses, or whoever was free and interested to join us in the work.

In the districts where there were no missionaries, we would try and camp in a village, perhaps in the courtyard of a Christian family, and take with us the Bible women loaned from other missions.

Mother of Hope was to spend one week of every month helping us, and another splendid Bible woman, Mother of Grace, and an evangelist from the same German mission, were to be freed to work with us several days each week. So that with hearts overflowing with praise and thankfulness, we realized that the promise was indeed coming true, we were running with the good news, and we could trust the One who went with us, to keep us from stumbling.

A few months later there came a day Faith and I will not forget. A letter had arrived for me just as we were starting off together in the car, and it was not until we were sitting on some rocks far away in the wilds, eating our mid-day picnic, that I had time to open the letter.

We could hardly believe that we were seeing correctly when we read that my father was sending us a third car, and that it was already on its way out to us. A third car! So that a third pair could go out preaching. There and then on the rocks we stood up and sang together the words which have become our familiar Fellowship Thanksgiving:

Praise God from whom all blessings flow,
Praise Him all creatures here below,
  Hallelujah, hallelujah,
Praise Him above, ye heavenly host,
Praise Father, Son and Holy Ghost,
  Hallelujah, hallelujah,
  Hallelujah, hallelujah,
    Hallelujah.

The cars of course made all the difference to our work, indeed without them we could not have attempted the great task before us. But we were now to discover what really difficult driving was like. The tracks to the villages in those days were truly awful. Very few had anything approaching to a road. They were mostly camel and donkey tracks, narrow, stony and often with jagged rocks sticking up all over them, and the way was often so narrow, that it was impossible to turn the car, and one simply had to go on and on whether the track came to an end or not.

    I think I hated and feared the mountain valleys more than anything else. It always seemed to me that the wheels must cease to grip on the loose stones. And at the bottom of most ravines, there would be the dry bed of a mountain torrent to negotiate, full of boulders and loose stones, and one either crashed against boulders or sank in the stones, and then everyone would have to get out and push.

    I was born with no mechanical instinct whatsoever, and the engine of my car was an awful and alarming mystery to me. And of course the Bible woman knew absolutely nothing at all about cars. In one way this was a very good thing, as they never appeared to be at all nervous or discouraged by any tracks or rough joltings, and though often my own hands were clammy with fright, they had the most touching confidence in my ability to drive them through or over anything.

It often took us several hours of exhausting driving to get within easy walking distance of a village, and I never quite got over the nightmare fear that the car would break down there, away in the wilds, and that I would be unable to make it start. The fact that this never happened in all the years of our village work, and that the few real break-downs we did suffer, all occured on main roads where help was quickly available, never availed to silence my fears.

The thought persistently haunted me, that the day would arrive when the Lord would test my faith by letting me have a real break-down in some awful, inaccessible spot; and though I was theoretically sure, that if that happened, He would in some way effect a rescue for us, and although I hated and abominated my own fear and unbelief, they persisted. It needed a definite act of surrender and faith, every single time, before I could start off on a trip which I could see from the survey map would mean encountering deep ravines and mountain tracks, or miles of sandy wastes where the car would stick.

I used to think how lovely it would be if the Lord would provide a male preacher to go with us, who was also a mechanic. But He only did this once, and on that occasion we broke down. In the end I began to realize that, the Lord being what He is, the weaker and feebler our little party was, the more certain we were to get safely and easily through.

On one occasion I had gone out with a particularly frail missionary to a certain Moslem village where the track was full of immense boulders, and a large party of the men of the village very kindly turned out to help us push and lift the car over these rocks. As I was putting the car away on our return home, a British policeman asked us where we had visited that day. When I told him the name of the village he looked horror-struck and exclaimed, "Surely not! We had to take our strongest armoured car there a day or two ago, and we broke our back axle on those rocks and were stranded hours and hours before we could be towed home. How on earth could you get your weak little car through?"

And once, during the war, when spare parts were no longer available, we were on our way to a village on the mountains near Safad, and I did not notice a deep pit at one side of the track. One of our front wheels went right down into this pit and there we were completely stuck. Some peasants working nearby came to our assistance, and at last managed to lift the front of the car up and get all four wheels on the road again. But we had gone down with such a bump, that the front outer spring was badly broken.

We managed to crawl back to Safad and stopped to enquire of a man the way to the garage. He was sympathetic but firmly pessimistic. "There is no place in this little town," he said, "where you can get that spring repaired. No spare parts are available in the place. You will have to crawl to Haifa about forty miles away, and get it mended there."

This was terrible news. It would take a whole day to reach Haifa with our broken spring and if, as had happened before under similar circumstances, the wheel got jammed, we should be stranded by the way. So immediately, while still sitting in the car, we had a time of prayer, and asked the Lord in some way to supply our needs. Then we drove to the one garage in the little town, to see if they could do anything for us.

I explained our situation to the owner of the garage, and he came out to examine the car. A peculiar expression crossed his face, and then he said:

"You have the most extraordinary luck. In the ordinary way I could have done nothing for you, but early this morning a lorry stopped here and the driver asked me if I wanted to buy some second hand spare parts, and some old iron junk he had. I was glad of the chance, and took all that he offered, and among the pieces which he left there is one spring from an Austin the very size you need."

Faith had one specially lovely experience with her car. She had gone out for a long day's trip into a very sandy wilderness near Gaza, with her Bible woman, who, although full of evangelistic zeal had a very weak heart and could not walk. From the moment of starting it was obvious to Faith that her engine was going to prove troublesome, but it was the last day of their trip, and one distant village remained to be reached. So she decided to make the attempt. The village was reached, after considerable difficulty, and the preaching faithfully carried out, and they started on the return journey. They had left the village a mile or two behind, and were several miles from the nearest main road, when she suddenly discovered her radiator was empty.

While she lay under the car endeavouring, but quite unsuccessfully, to plug the leak, the Bible woman sat by the track and prayed for help. The afternoon began to draw to a close. They were out on a lonely desert. Nobody passed along the track at that hour, for everyone tried to be in the safety of their homes by nightfall. There was no car in the lonely village they had left, and no bus ever passed along that track. Faith decided to try by creeping a few yards at a time, and then stopping to cool the engine, to reach the nearest village. But she quickly realized this was impossible.

Suddenly the Bible woman exclaimed, "Just look! A car is coming behind us." It drew up and out stepped a well dressed Arab gentleman who spoke to them in perfect English. They explained the plight they were in, and with the utmost courtesy he said he would be delighted to tow them to the main road. He not only did this, but insisted on towing them on to the nearest town.

It was quite dark by then and he took them to a garage. He himself still had a journey of several hours ahead of him, but he insisted on carrying their bags to a hotel he himself could recommend.

As he was leaving he said, again with great courtesy, for both Faith and the Bible woman were dusty and dishevelled and very much the rather impoverished looking missionary, "I hope you will forgive me if I ask if you have enough to pay for your night's lodgings?"

They were able to assure him that they had, and then Faith said, "I would so much like to ask you one question before you go. We were told that village does not possess a single car, how did you happen to come along that solitary track at such a late hour, just as we were praying for help?"

"It is indeed very remarkable," he replied, "and if I may say so you were extraordinarily fortunate. There is no car in that village, and there is no likelihood at all that anyone able to help you would have passed by. You would either have had to pass the night in your car, or have walked back to the village. I myself had business which took me there, and I arranged with the head man to sleep there all night.

"We finished our business sooner than I had expected, and as I was very tired I lay down at once to sleep. Just before sunset I suddenly woke up, and feeling quite rested I decided for some unknown reason, and in spite of the protests of my host, to drive straight home to Jerusalem (a long journey) instead of spending the night there as arranged. And thus I was most opportunely able to come to your assistance."

"Ah!" exclaimed the Bible woman, "we know why you woke just then. We were praying for help and God woke you and sent you to our aid."

One missionary friend at an earlier stage, had dubbed these outings to the villages, "holy picnics." We were all a little indignant when we first heard our wearisome and difficult journeys thus described. We discussed it together in a somewhat martyrlike way, and decided it was a sad misnomer.

"Everyone thinks the same thing," said one of the Bible women. "When I start off with you for a week's trip to the villages, my grown-up children say, 'Hello, here's mother going off for another picnic. How lucky you are. We have to stay here in this hot city of Haifa and work and endure air-raids, and we are not even able to go out for excursions in our free time because of the dangerous situation in the country. And here you are riding about all over the country and having a fine time.' They just don't understand how difficult these journeys are, and that it is certainly no picnic to sit down and preach to a lot of fanatical men."

"And I certainly don't think its much of a picnic driving an old car, constantly needing repairs, over these ghastly tracks, and wondering if we shall ever get home again, or if we shall be blown up by a land mine, or be shot," said I. "And think of the miles we have to tramp in the hot sun, and not even able to drink a glass of water when we get to a village. We are sadly misunderstood, if people think we are all on a picnic when we are invading Satan's stronghold."

But Faith would have none of this martyr attitude, and bluntly prodded us to truthful confession.

"I think there's a lot of truth in the name," she said. "We do have lovely times, and we would all of us much rather be doing this work than being stuck in the towns.

"In spite of difficult driving and heat and thirst and tiredness, we do all enjoy it tremendously. And when we finish the preaching, it is a picnic. Our friends see us come home loaded with wild flowers and wild salads that we have collected on the mountains, and they see us full of joy and praise over the opportunities we have had in the villages, and they know nothing about the real battling part of it, and it's no wonder they think we have good times and envy us. I think 'holy picnics' rather well describes it. First the battle and then the rejoicing, and not one of us would change places with our friends at home."

And we were all honestly obliged to agree with her. The Bible women did actually love the work as much as we did, and looked forward to the trips with joy. In spring especially, we had the most delightful times on the way home, gathering masses of wild flowers. And the Bible women taught us the names and uses of the wild green things growing on the hills so that we seldom returned without delicious salads and mountain greens to cook for vegetables.

12

"IN THE PATHS
OF DEATH
THEY ROAM"

"Without Christ . . . having no hope, and without God in the world" (Eph. 2:12).

It was now my joy to be able to return to the Jordan Valley where Hope and I had visited the pioneer villages during the first year of our work. But this time we went in order to preach to the Bedouin tribesmen themselves, and to visit their scattered encampments, a task which three years before I would never have dreamed possible.

I have paid many long visits to Beisan at various times, and eventually it became my home and I have come to love it more than any other part of the country, and because it has become so specially dear to me I have been tempted into fuller description.

More and more I came to love the peaceful little mission compound with its tiny garden full of pomegranate trees and olive saplings, the giant fig trees whose leaves tapped against the windows of the guest room, the brawling stream racing past the bottom of the garden, and the kingfishers with their brilliant plumage, swooping from tree to tree.

It was wild and lonely country all round the little garden. The jackals howled round the houses night after night, and down in the banana plantations and it was no uncommon thing for wild boar to be hunted. Occasionally there would be rumours of a hyena in the neighbourhood, but these creatures more hated and feared even than leopards, were becoming rarer and rarer. Leopards and lions had once, not so long ago, haunted the valley and the neighbouring mountains, but had been driven away.

In spring immense flocks of storks broke their journey in the valley, and although most of them only remained a few weeks, there were smaller flocks which remained the whole year round, and it was a beautiful picture on some stormy, winter evening, to see these huge birds roosting on the flowery mimosa trees, their white plumage and the mass of yellow flowers, shining white and gold against the black banks of clouds.

Frogs of course were everywhere, in every puddle, stream and bog, making the nights noisy with their croaking. The dogs barked and howled more incessantly in this little town than in any other village I ever stayed in. They seemed to band together in packs at night, and there was war and uproar beside every garbage heap in the place. On nights when the moon was full there was pandemonium.

The whole valley itself, was marshy and malarious, and travelling was extremely difficult. There were lakes and ponds and endless streams. Multitudes of water fowl of all kinds haunted it. It was beautiful to watch the wild geese and ducks flying overhead in their own peculiar formations. Towards evening the eastern mountains turned rose pink and mauve, the western ones turned indigo blue and black, and often across a fiery red or golden sky above these dark mountains, the wild birds in spear or arrow shaped formations, made a picture never to be forgotten.

At that time there were no proper roads at all, and it seemed as though sooner or later a stream or marsh intercepted every track we followed. Sometimes it was possible to drive through, often, impossible. The tribes moved from place to place and therefore there were no permanent tracks which could be depended upon to bring us to their tents, though there were places where they stored their grain and left certain of their possessions. The better tracks generally led us to some such deserted place, a group of half ruined store houses, with perhaps one decrepit old man in charge, and then the black tents themselves would be descried several miles further on.

More than once when we drove towards these tents we found a wide sweep of river or rushing torrent, between them and us. And then it was necessary to leave the car and find a shallow spot and wade across. In the north of Palestine, in the marshy districts around Lake Huleh (the ancient waters of Mirom), we encountered the same difficulties in an even more aggravated form and most of our visiting had to be done on horseback.

I

was once visiting in the Huleh district with a keen
Christian nurse from the Tiberias Mission Hospitals, who went with me to act as interpreter. We
came to a very wide, but comparatively shallow
river, between us and our destination. So we took
off our shoes and stockings and waded across. As
we came up from the river right into the village and
were very wet and muddy, and an interested crowd
had gathered to watch us make the crossing, I
thought we should be very ill advised to sit down
in front of everyone and put our stockings on
again, and on this occasion therefore, I thought fit
to waive the strict rule that when visiting in these
villages our legs and arms must be covered in order
not to shock Moslem decorum.

So we padded with
bare black legs to the village meeting place and sat
down among the women and tried to begin our
preaching. But it was a mistake. One old lady after
staring with great disapproval, interrupted the
preaching to say disgustedly: "How dare you come
to visit us with your flesh thus showing?"

Very
crestfallen we explained that we had but just come
up from a very muddy river, and hoped that they
would excuse us that we had not put on our
stockings again. But we saw that the excuse was
inadequate, and we were obliged then and there to
pull out our stockings and don them again, before
we could decently continue the preaching.

As far
as we could discover, none of these villages or
encampments in the Beisan district had ever been

visited by preachers of the gospel. We were quite literally the first to bring them the good news of the Saviour. But the ignorance and spiritual darkness of the people were so intense, it was fearfully difficult to know how to present the message in a way to make any kind of appeal to them. The women especially seemed very degraded and almost like animals.

Later on when I lived in Beisan I once went to visit a Christian on the outskirts of the town. On an open piece of ground nearby, there was a group of black tents belonging to some tribespeople who had pitched temporarily near the market town. I saw a ragged, wild looking man come dashing along on a horse. The reins were flung over one arm, and with that hand he held a rope, to which was tethered a young woman, hardly more than a child. He alternately lashed the horse and then the woman tethered to the rope, so that she was forced to run at full speed, panting and sobbing, in order to keep up with the horse and escape being dragged helplessly along the ground.

We went over to the tents to expostulate, and found the girl like a wild trapped animal, panting, trembling and unable to say a word. The other women had collected around and were slapping and scolding her. They told us that she was married to a man who ill treated her, and every night she tried to run away, and someone was forced to ride after her and bring her back.

As we visited the homes in this Moslem town, and listened to the stories of the women, who are all smiles and apparently quite happy when they first received us, it was pathetic to see how quickly that aspect changed when we started talking to them and won their confidence. What stories they poured out. It seemed as though there was not one home where stark tragedy was absent. And the suffering due to ignorance, superstition, and lack of medical help was simply appalling.

In those earlier years there was no doctor in the place. And here as in every other district it happened more than once that during our visits to remote villages, we were able to drive sick people back with us to a hospital, who would otherwise have been left to die in the village, or would have been forced to travel for hours sitting on a donkey. The matron of the Nablus Mission Hospital told me, that one day a maternity case from a remote village arrived at the hospital, the woman having been carried all the way in her coffin. Fortunately after an operation she made an excellent recovery, and coffin and happy mother returned to the village separately.

On one occasion we met an anxious group on a distant track. A girl had just been bitten by a poisonous snake and they were miles away from any help. We rushed her to the nearest hospital, and she also made a good recovery.

In such ways we were able to show practical help and sympathy, and the number of lifts given to villagers who were heavily burdened, was legion. It was pleasant if we overtook a man on the way to the village we were going to, as we could then give him a lift, and count on his helping to give us a good welcome on arrival in the village.

One day when I had gone out by myself to a quiet hillside for prayer, a crowd of Arab women and children arrived, intent on a picnic, and in their usual friendly way, they came and sat down beside me and began asking a great many questions about myself and where I came from. Alas, I was so intent on having my quiet time that I resented their presence. I told them, rather ungraciously, that I had come out to that quiet place because I wished to be alone, and would be grateful if they would go and sit a little further away. There was plenty of room on the hill for us all.

As always happens, my ungracious manner provoked ungraciousness in return. They refused to move, and the boys began throwing stones at my dog, and the more I commanded them to move away, the more teasing and rude they became.

How different it might have been if only I had let them sit with me a little while and satisfied their friendly and natural curiosity. They would then, quite willingly, have moved away later on. But I became more and more exasperated and angry. And all the time, though I was so irritated that I would not think about it, I knew that the Lord was there and was being hurt, and that if they had seen Him there, praying alone, and had sat down beside Him, what a different reception He would have given them.

At last, after I had threatened for some time and got really angry, they moved off and left me alone with the Lord who said to me, "Oh Grace, I did so want you to speak to those poor women, and you have driven them away." I was overwhelmed with shame and sorrow, but it was too late, the crowd was already out of sight. But my prayer time was absolutely spoiled. I knew I had disappointed the Lord and missed an opportunity which He had given me. I confessed my sorrow and shame and asked that if possible I might be granted another opportunity to speak to that group I had driven away. Then I got up sadly and went home.

And just outside our house, to my unspeakable joy, I met the same group of women and children, who, when they saw me, began to point and call out rude remarks. But I was beyond caring, and so thankful for a second opportunity, that I hurried up to them and exclaimed, "Oh I am so sorry and ashamed that I spoke to you as I did this morning, and drove you away. Please don't think that the Lord Jesus would have done the same. And please forgive me."

The whole crowd gathered round me in happy and surprised delight. The boys dropped their stones and began to smile. And all the women began to pat me on the back and say that of course they had not really minded. And one of them put her arm round me and said, "Don't be sorry. We did not mean to trouble you. But when I saw you sitting there, and saw that you were a Christian, because my heart is very sad and lonely, I wanted to speak to you. Will you come and visit me in my house?"

Joy and shame struggled in me as I stood there in the main street of our town, and this woman, a complete stranger, stood with her arm around me, telling me of her need and longing for my help, and realizing that I had actually driven her away when the Lord had brought her to me. I promised that we would visit her as soon as possible. And a day or two later the Bible woman and I went to her little mud hut. And there she told us her story.

She was the daughter of a Christian man of one of the wealthier villages, in which her family held a leading position. When she was about eighteen, her brother, who was the head of the family, fell in love with a Moslem woman in a neighbouring village, and persuaded her to marry him without her parents' consent. This was considered a terrible crime and a blood feud was imminent. The woman's family however agreed to pass over the matter if the man would pay a large sum of money, and also give one of his Christian sisters in marriage to a son of the Moslem family who had been wronged, in order to even things up.

The poor woman who was telling us the tale was the sister chosen. She absolutely refused to marry the man, but her brother actually forced her to do so at the point of the gun, in order to save himself from death. She therefore found herself married to a man who already had a wife, and there was not a single Christian in his village. The first wife was terribly jealous and having no children herself, this jealousy flamed into passionate hatred when the new wife gave birth to a son. Several times she tried to poison the young Christian wife, and at last the husband decided to send her and his little son to live in the town, where he could visit them frequently, and where they would be free from the murderous attempts of his other wife.

And when she had finished her tale of suffering and loneliness, and of the long years cut off from all intercourse with her Christian people, she looked up and said pathetically, "It is fifteen years since I have heard the name of Jesus. That is why I so wanted to come and speak to you, when I saw you sitting on the hill, though I would not have dared to say anything of this to you in front of the other women. Now tell me more about Him. I have forgotten all I ever learnt."

I think that never in my life have I felt so rebuked and ashamed. How nearly, but for the Lord's loving grace in letting us meet again, I had missed the opportunity of making contact with this sorrowful and longing soul. And all because I had wanted the luxury of spending an uninterrupted time with the Lord in prayer, and had not wanted to share my blessings at that moment with the poor women.

This woman, whom we met in this remarkable way, came to visit us frequently, whenever possible joining us at the simple morning prayer and Bible reading which we held daily before breakfast. Later on she was recalled to her husband's village. We shall never forget her last words and the wistful look in her eyes as she said, "Do you really believe that He will be able to keep me and help me when I am all alone back there in our village?"

One day during our stay in Beisan when we got back after a day's visiting amongst the tribesmen, we were told that a young Moslem woman who had been coming to the little clinic at the mission station had just given birth to a baby. She was in a desperately serious condition, however, and the only hope of saving her life was to get her to a hospital as soon as possible. But the nearest hospital was about twenty miles away in Nazareth.

It was just sunset, and after sunset there was curfew on the roads all over the country because of terrorist gangs who during the years 1936-39 were almost nightly intent on deeds of violence. But as it was a desperate case I was asked if I were willing to drive this woman and the midwife to the hospital, and of course I gladly agreed. The woman's husband insisted on coming with us, and we took the two-hour-old baby, tightly swaddled, and away we went.

It was quite dark, and as there was curfew the track was of course completely deserted. It was terribly rough and bumpy, for a proper road at that time had not been made, but it was urgent to get to the hospital as soon as possible. It was the strangest ride of my life. The headlights picked out the rough track ahead and illuminated occasional trees at the road-side. Finally we reached a main road and sped towards a range of high hills, on top of which was the town of Nazareth and our nearest mission hospital.

Just as we came to the foot of these hills, the full moon rose over Mount Tabor on our right, flooding the whole landscape with silvery light. And at that moment the young mother in the back of the car became unconscious. The husband lost all control of himself, and fell shrieking on top of his wife. The midwife thrust the swaddled baby she had been holding into my arms.

While she was trying to tear the husband off the young mother, I, with the baby in one arm, was searching frantically for a piece of iron we could force between the clenched teeth of the dying woman. Then I laid the baby on the empty seat beside me and, supporting her with one hand, began the ascent of the hairpin bends up the mountain, urging the car forward as fast as possible. At that moment I was so vividly conscious of the presence of the Lord Jesus Himself, that it seemed He was almost visible. Up and up the car twisted, myself trying to take the agonizing sharp bends with one hand on the wheel, the other holding the baby on the slippery seat.

The whole scene is fixed in my memory like an over-exposed photograph, in sharp blacks and whites, the dark mountains and the hairpin bends of the road white in the moonlight, the cries of the husband behind, the midwife urging me to drive faster, and the helpless baby sliding on the seat beside me. But just as clear cut, and all part of the same nightmare scene, was a strange object which suddenly darted across the road in the glare of the headlights, looking at first like a ghostly turkey with a huge transparent tail spread fanwise. Then I saw that it was a giant porcupine with all its quills erected as it scuttled across the road.

And so at last we came to the town on the mountain top, and drove up to the door of the hospital. I took the swaddled baby and hurried inside, and in a moment or two the doctor and his stretcher bearers came and lifted out the unconscious woman.

She was laid on the operating table and died that very moment. The long agonizing ride had been in vain. This woman had died without hearing of Christ the Saviour. I was still clutching her newborn baby in my arms, and her husband was sobbing in despair beside us. At that moment I turned in silence to the Lord, with an almost desperate questioning of the heart.

"Why did you let us make such an effort to save this woman's body, and yet give her no opportunity to hear the message of life? Where has she gone now? Is there any use at all in all our mission work? She is just one among a multitude of other souls leaving this world in ignorance and darkness. Only she died among Christians, and yet never had an opportunity to hear of Christ."

And it seemed to me that in answer to this desperate questioning of the heart, the Lord said, "Grace, you are conscious of Me here beside you now. All that long journey in the car you knew My presence with you. When this poor ignorant woman's soul passed out of her body, I was here beside you both. Cannot you trust her to Me and My love? Will you not believe that nothing has been left undone, nor will be left undone, that can help her? Trust her to me. My cross is the sign that My love

128

will do all that is possible to save every single soul, the darkest and most ignorant as well as the most privileged."

This experience made a lasting impression on me. It was not that I felt afterwards that it did not matter so much if we did not urgently seek the lost before they left this world, for in the end all will be well. Rather, it was an overwhelming sense of our Lord's passionate love and longing for the souls of all whom He has created, and His determination to seek them at all costs, and His longing that we should co-operate with Him in this work. The one thing we cannot do, we who have tasted of His love and grace, and been lifted out of the darkness, and brought into all the joy and power of knowing Him, is to sit back comfortably and leave Him alone in His task of searching for the lost.

Next morning when it was time to return home, I found the doctor expostulating with the young husband of the dead woman. The man said he was too poor to hire a hearse and drive his dead wife home, but she must not be buried in Christian ground or among Christians. What was to be done? The man turned to me, imploring me to drive her home again. I had never supposed that it was possible or permissible to drive an uncoffined body in a private car, but the doctor told me that it was permissible if I had the death certificate, and if I were willing to do it. It seemed the only way to manage, so I agreed.

The dead woman was carried out wrapped in blankets, all prepared for burial, and was placed in the back of the open car. Her husband crouched on the floor beside her, weeping and calling her by name and imploring her to speak to him. Her baby girl remained behind to be cared for by the hospital. Mile after mile as we drove along, we heard the poor man in the back, caressing his wife, calling her every endearing name he could think of, and imploring her to answer him.

A mile or two outside his home town we came to a group of workmen mending the road, and the husband suddenly shouted to me, "Stop the car." He said two of the workmen were his relatives, and they must come to assist at the funeral, which, according to the laws of the land, had to take place the same day as death. I expostulated saying that there was no room in the car, but he said he would tell them that she had died, and they would take a short cut to the house. Meanwhile he seized their two spades, and we drove the rest of the way to their poverty-stricken cottage, bearing with us not only the body to be buried, but the spades for digging her grave.

The neighbours all came out weeping and wailing, to meet us, and when the body had been lifted from the car, wrapped in blankets and ready to be buried just as it was, we turned sorrowfully away.

13
THE LAST LAP

"Faithful is He that calleth you, Who also will do it" (I Thess. 5:24).

Towards the end of the fourth year, I was able during the rainy season, to spend a term at language school in Jerusalem, a thing I had yearned to do ever since starting work among the Moslem villages. For, although I had very soon begun to find, after sitting for hours on the floors of hundreds of village guest rooms, that I could understand almost all the preaching in Arabic, the actual questions asked, and the remarks made by the people themselves, were still unintelligible to me. But of course it was quite impossible for me to take any real part in the conversation myself, except by interpretation.

This opportunity for being silent onlooker and listener, proved invaluable in one way. I learned to notice very quickly how the people reacted to the different methods of preaching the gospel, and became very sensitive to the atmosphere, and to reading the faces before us. But I knew that what I really needed was definite teaching, and when this opportunity to spend a term at language school studying Arabic arrived, I was overjoyed. The Second World War was raging and already parts for the car were nearly unobtainable and petrol strictly rationed, so that it seemed an excellent opportunity to take a term at school and save petrol for later on.

Language school was a great luxury. No responsibility, no wrestling with bad roads, no wearisome tramps in the heat, nothing to do but enjoy the opportunity of learning the language I needed so much, with the help of expert teachers, and to revel in the fellowship of other missionaries. All of a sudden life became easy and comfortable and restful. It is true that we went out faithfully one afternoon each week, to villages in the neighbourhood, but they were within easy reach, and entailed only pleasure and no fatigue.

As the weeks passed by, the happy life at language school became more and more attractive, and the thought of returning to the struggle to reach every place, during the coming hot months, seemed less and less supportable. Surely there was no great hurry? I had been travelling incessantly for four and a half years, and latterly visiting two or three villages a day.

Faith was still faithfully struggling in the south, while I was enjoying language school, but in a week or two all the first round to every place in her district would be finished. Would it matter if I waited until the autumn to finish mine? And would it not really be much better to concentrate on the language for at least another term? I should be able to do better work afterwards. Still about a hundred places remained to be reached, before we could say that every single place in the country had been visited with the gospel message at least once. And those hundred places were all in the most difficult and inaccessible areas, and would involve some of the longest journeys and the most difficult driving yet experienced.

And so I decided to postpone until the autumn the finishing of the task the Lord had called me to. I would stay at language school another term, and also take the short summer course, and then I would tackle the remaining hundred places.

One evening towards the end of term, I went out alone for a quiet time with the Lord on a hillside. It was a favourite spot of mine; a hilltop from which one looked out over range after range of other hills and shadowy valleys, the hills dwindling gradually in height until they reached the plain, and in the far distance the blue Mediterranean shining in the sunlight. It was just towards sunset. The sky turned fiery red and the distant scene changed from misty blue to gold and rose. And then the stars came out one by one and the long ranges of hills turned dark and gloomy.

Little lights began to twinkle on their slopes, and the glow of camp fires. All those lights on the darkening hills represented villages we had visited. I pictured them one by one as night fell, all the innumerable little mud houses, with darkness coming down on the sorrows and fears and pains and sins of so many Christless homes. I knew something about the life in each of those Moslem places. I knew a little of what the coming of darkness meant in so many of the homes. And I began to pray desperately for the people of the villages and towns as the night swallowed them up. Then I seemed to hear the Lord say, "Grace, it is time to finish the task. The night cometh when no man can work."

I said, "Lord, let me rest a little longer, and finish in the autumn."

He said, "No. I have set before you an open door, and no man can shut it. But the task must be finished while it is still open."

I was horrified to find how unattractive the thought of the work had grown to my mind during the past three months. I shrank from the labour and strain involved in finishing it. And as always, a sense of terrible weakness and helplessness swept over me. The Lord never seemed to ask one to do things one felt fit or able for.

Then, as I stared out on the dimly twinkling lights, I noticed the infinite strength and stability on the hills on which these countless villages were built. The villages themselves were so small and comparatively frail, while the hills so immovably, so calmly and majestically, bore up without strain or weariness, everything built or growing or supported on them. Was not God's strength just like that? If one but rested on Him, weakness and feebleness were nothing. His was the responsibility, and His the power to support and bear and carry.

So the last lap was started. It was the most difficult of all. A large number of unreached places still remained on the lower foothills in the central districts of Nablus and Lydda. God gave me as companion a young Christian woman full of zeal and enthusiasm, and what was, at that stage, of equal importance, a good walker, a rare accomplishment in town dwellers.

She went out with me week after week. We stayed with a wonderfully kind Christian family in Tulkarm. There was no mission station in the whole district. It was appallingly hot and the sandflies and mosquitoes were cruel. I hardly know what we would have done if it had not been watermelon season, and the watermelon district. We had longer and rougher walks than in any other district, the tracks being so stony that our shoes fell to pieces. But on arrival at every village we could be pretty certain of being offered large refreshing chunks of watermelon.

But the people in those villages were not easy to visit, in fact they were more difficult than any others. They were constantly quarrelling with neighbouring settlements, especially those belonging to people of a different religion. On more than one occasion we were in danger of being stoned, until we could satisfy the people that we were not Jews!

The whole memory of those visits is blurred and indistinct; it seemed one long wrestle with heat and weariness and stony tracks on treeless hills, and of returning to our Christian friends in the evening, too tired to eat. We wanted nothing but drink after drink.

I was allowed to put my little camp bed in the tiny courtyard at night, but it was too hot to sleep, and the sandflies penetrated my net, and all night seemed to be spent tossing on the narrow bed and drinking glass after glass of water.

The first week we had a Bible woman with us, but after one day's visiting in the heat she had a very bad heart attack, and we realized she must return home. How thankfully I rejoiced in the faithful friendship and support of Joy. She wore out her own shoes on those awful stone tracks, and then tramped day after day in an old pair of my village shoes which were far too large for her. She never grumbled nor compalined, always did her preaching with a radiant face, and what was still more wonderful to me, was always willing to sit up every night talking to the Christian and non-Christian visitors who came to the house, witnessing to them. And she did not have a very easy time.

For though it was accepted by the people of the town that a foreign missionary might wander about preaching in the villages, it was something quite new for a young Christian woman of the country to do the same, and Joy was frequently told that she ought to stay at home and help her mother or sisters-in-law. Her mother, however, was an earnest Christian woman, and gladly set her free for this work, and Joy was quite literally the only companion who could have helped me finish the work in that district, for she was the only one among our little band of helpers who had the language and was also strong enough for much walking.

Thus once again God wonderfully fulfilled His promise and supplied all our needs. The door was still open and the ideal companion forthcoming.

At long last we finished that district and went up the mountains to Jerusalem again, for a few weeks rest. During the past few months I had lost over a stone in weight and was very weary. It seemed impossible to reach the last villages before autumn. A friend however came to visit me. She said that she was free, and that it had been laid upon her heart that she and I together should camp in a tiny Christian village in the heart of the Nablus area where the last unreached villages were. I told her that I was very sorry, but I felt I could not face any more visiting during the hot weather. She was very persistent however, and we agreed to pray about the matter.

The very next morning I met another friend on the street, and he said at once, "Oh how sorry I am that this new regulation has been passed that all civilian cars must be taken off the roads by the fifteenth of this month. I am afraid that means that you cannot finish getting to every place in the country."

I stood as though thunderstruck. Could it possibly be true? Was the door, which over and over again had seemed to be closing, and which God had kept open for five years, really going to be shut at last? How thankful I was that we had not put off the finishing of our task until the autumn. But even now it was impossible to finish the work in the few days remaining to us.

I hurried off to my friend and told her the dreadful news. We had prayer together, and then sent in an application to the authorities asking for a two months extension of the time for using our car, in order to finish our work of reaching every place in the country. To our amazement and joy this permission was granted, and we were also granted new tyres for the car (a second miracle), and all the petrol we asked for!

Three of us went out day after day, in a last desperate effort to reach all the villages, and in the end we did reach all of them except thirty. But the friend who had invited me to Nablus undertook to visit these remaining villages on donkey back, and she actually did manage to do this during the following autumn and winter.

Thus what had seemed at the beginning such a stupendous and impossible task, was actually accomplished. Every single place in Palestine, as far as we knew, had been visited once at least. The gospel message had been preached in all, and the printed Word of God had been left behind. It had taken just five years to finish the work. And God had most wonderfully supplied every single need: all the literature in the many necessary different languages; large free grants of Bibles; and thousands of Testaments. All the travelling expenses had been supplied, we hardly knew how, and above all, the necessary helpers and preachers had been raised up.

Health and strength sufficient for the

task had been granted to all of us, although almost all the messengers had been physically very feeble folk. Not one of us had contracted any of the maladies so common in the villages, though constantly exposed to infection. In all the thousands of miles of difficult travel we had been spared from accident and from violence, and from all serious breakdowns, and our daily experiences of the Lord's wonderful care and kindness, had made life a continual joyful adventure. And above all, every single place in the country had been opened to the preaching of the gospel. We were surely the most privileged people in the land.

14
THE CHALLENGE

"I heard the voice of the Lord saying, 'Whom shall I send and who will go for us?' Then said I, 'Here am I, send me'" (Isa. 6:8).

So the last day came. We packed up our camping equipment, and after driving my friend back to her home I started off alone in the car to the home base, where the car which had served us so wonderfully, was to be stored until the arrival of better days.

As I drove back over the mountains alone, I was very conscious of the presence of the Wayfarer Who had called us just five years before to the task, which by His wonderful grace and help, we had just finished. How full of unspeakable joy and blessing, along with conflict, those five years had been, how rich in new friendships, how full of joyful service. A verse which Faith often quoted came into my mind:

"I will worship towards Thy holy temple, and praise Thy name for Thy loving kindness and for Thy truth, for Thou hast magnified Thy word above all Thy name" (Psalm 138:2).

Our Lord had indeed done for us far more than we had asked or thought possible. "He is faithful that promised." "All the promises of God in Him are yea and amen."

As the Wayfarer and I drove together for the last time before the car must be taken off the road, I looked out on the villages and mountain tracks, leading to them, every one of which we had come to know so well, and the joy of fulfilment was suddenly swallowed up in pain. So many of them—and only visited once. Surely this could not be the end, but only the beginning of something far better and greater.

I stopped the car in a lonely place and turned to the Wayfarer Who had called and led us out to follow Him to every place.

"Surely this can't be the end!" I cried desperately. "This can't be the last time that we shall go out together to these places. Promise me that soon we may start again. 'Oh Thou Who art the hope of Israel, the Saviour thereof in time of trouble, why shouldst Thou be as a stranger in the land? As a wayfaring man that turneth aside to tarry but a night? Why shouldst Thou be as one that cannot save?' (Jer. 14:8). Lord raise up and send out a band of witnesses that all these villages may be visited again and again until Thou art welcomed in all of them as Saviour."

"While there are still lost sheep," said the Wayfarer, "I will never rest from seeking them."

A rush of unspeakable joy flooded my heart. "Then Lord, we will still go with Thee. Lead on and we will follow. This is not the end of the search, but only the beginning."

> Mine are the hands to do Thy work,
> My feet shall run for Thee,
> My lips shall sound the glorious news,
> Lord here am I, send me.

That is why this little book has been written. Perhaps there are others who will hear the Wayfarer calling them out to search with Him in His unresting work of going after the lost.

> Oh come let us go and find them,
> In the paths of death they roam,
> At the close of the day, 'twill be sweet to say
> I have brought some lost one home.

15
POSTSCRIPT
Our Inescapable Responsibility

It is told of a certain missionary bishop, that he was once asked by a young candidate for the foreign field, what, in his opinion, was the best preparation and training a prospective missionary could undergo during his last year in the home land. The bishop replied that he considered the best possible preparation would be to speak to as many individual people as possible, about their personal relationship to the Lord Jesus Christ.

I was reminded of this quite recently when talking to a young missionary just arrived on the field, and beginning her language study before going on to teach in a mission school. After asking some questions about the evangelistic work in the villages, she said quite simply and rather wistfully, "I shouldn't even know how to begin talking to anyone about spiritual things. I have no experience at all in such matters." And when I asked why, in that case, she had joined a missionary society, and come to the mission field, she replied that she hoped by teaching in the school, and by personal kindness, to influence the girls under her care to desire a higher standard of life, and to appreciate the superiority of Christianity over every other religion.

This very attractive young woman, seems typical of a large number of new recruits coming to the mission field. Experience and skill in personally announcing the good news, and engaging in what is known as personal work, is no longer considered an indispensable qualification in a missionary.

At the first missionary conference which I myself attended on the mission field, nearly twenty years ago, a paper was read on "Institutionalism Versus Evangelism." During the discussion which followed, a remark was made with which the main body of missionaries appeared to be in agreement. It was claimed that, direct evangelism was so commonly left to well-meaning but tactless and ill-equipped workers, that it usually resulted in influencing one person at the expense of driving away and antagonizing ninty-nine others. And it was maintained that such a result did not justify the method.

I do not remember anyone rising to suggest that such a vitally important part of missionary work should not be left to tactless and ill-equipped workers, but should be definitely engaged in by all missionaries as an indispensable part of their work. But later experience has led me to believe that the answer would have been, either that mission stations are usually so understaffed and the pressure of work so great, that the average missionary has neither the time nor strength to engage in it; or else the simple confession that the missionary did not feel a gift or call to such work, and preferred quietly, by life and conduct, and sacrificial service, to influence the non-Christians around, and hoped that such a witness would not be in vain.

In some areas of the mission field this attitude on the part of the missionaries, coupled with the fact that there appears to be so little knowledge among Christians in non-Christian lands, as to how to set about personal evangelistic work, has meant that evangelism in the sense of personal fishing for men, is quietly dying out.

This seems to imply a misunderstanding or forgetfulness of our Lord's express command that His followers should go and preach His good news to every creature. Surely we cannot deny that it has been direct evangelism, that is to say, plainly announcing the good news of the gospel, backed up certainly, and supported by healing and teaching, which has produced all that is vital and lasting in Christianity wherever it is found in the world today.

It is the message of the living Saviour, and the leading into personal contact with Him, which saves and transforms men and women, and triumphs over the powers of evil in the world. This saving knowledge of the Son of God is the right of all who will believe His message. "But how shall they believe in Him of Whom they have not heard? And how shall they hear without a preacher?"

If the foreign missionary who has come to the mission field on purpose to announce the Evangel, is often so unpractised in the art of fishing for men, is it any wonder that the Christians themselves, who are always a small minority, should in so many cases, reveal the same inexperience? Indeed in large areas of the world the small Christian groups have lived so long in fear of persecution at the hands of their non-Christian neighbours, that it is become a deeply rooted idea that non-Christians cannot be converted, and that all attempts to try and persuade them to change their religion should be abandoned as useless and dangerous.

Thus countless numbers of potential fishers neglect altogether this most glorious of life's responsibilities, the joyful service of seeking to help men and women to a transforming knowledge of the Saviour of the world.

It must also be confessed with sorrow, that it is not only the new missionary coming to the foreign field, who sometimes lacks efficiency and experience in personal evangelism. But it does happen that professional evangelists or Bible women or missionaries of many years standing, may lack a vital element in their preaching. We evangelists, do also very easily fall into the habit of preaching a set of truths or doctrines designated as fundamental, or even as preaching Christ crucified, or the atonement, without perceiving that we have failed most lamentably to make it a real and living message to our hearers. That is to say we failed to make contact with their heart and conscience.

Our words seem like little stones peppering a massive

146

outer wall without penetrating anywhere near the inner citadel. What we say may be perfectly true and good, but it gets nowhere because it does not convey anything at all to our hearers. With our own Christian background so strongly influencing us, we easily fail to recognize that the mind of a non-Christian is likely to remain blankly indifferent and unresponsive to ideas and expressions of truth which touch us, personally, to the very depth of our being. The message we preach may speak to us, but it finds no way of entrance to them. It is all true, but powerless.

Anyone who out of a full heart and passionate desire to awaken a response to the love of God, has tried to preach the gospel, for example to a Moslem, has experienced this bitter feeling of defeat, as though he were beating against a blank wall. The awful tragedy of our work on the mission field is that so often we do not know how to engage or touch the hearts of our hearers. How often during the war we read that our Navy or Army had failed to engage the enemy or make contact with them. Equipment, striking power, all may have been excellent, but they were useless because they got nowhere near the target.

As I have sat on the floor of guest room after guest room in the villages, listening to a great variety of preaching by both men and women, and have watched the faces of our listeners, it has often seemed to me that we were failing completely to re-state the glorious truths of the gospel in a way which appealed to the non-Christian mind and to the very ignorant. Though the preaching may have been orthodox, and better still (to my mind) interesting, it did not strike any kind of response.

The reason for this is not that the gospel does not fit human needs today, nor suit the modern intellect, but simply that we have not sufficiently adapted our own understanding of these vital truths, and the words and phrases in which we express them, so that they will strike some spark of response in the hearts and consciences of those to whom we are preaching. This seems to be one of the most prevalent and tragic causes of our failure in evangelistic work, and the reason why direct evangelism has fallen into such disrepute.

It is not seldom that one hears the confident and self-congratulatory remark after preaching, "I gave the complete message and put before them the whole plan of salvation. Now the responsibility is theirs and I have delivered by soul." Alas, no, if that excellent description of the whole plan of salvation never penetrated further than the ears, never got anywhere near the citadel of the will, where some degree at least of acceptance or rejection must take place, never even provoked curiosity or after-thought, the responsibility is not entirely with the hearer, but at least equally with the tragically inefficient messenger who failed to find any kind of entrance for the Word.

Too much of our evangelistic preaching is like trying to force a large parcel of rich and valuable content into the tiny slit of a letter box, and when it will not go in, accusing the owner of the house of rejecting it.

Thank God, the gospel of the living Christ, is very adaptable, and without forfeiting any part of it, least of all the central core, which is the redeeming death of the Son of God, it can be so presented that it slips right into the heart and conscience of the hearer, where it will provoke some reaction, interest, response, dislike or rejection. The response made to it there is not our responsibility, but until our message has at least touched some point of inner sensitiveness, we have failed.

In the gospels we see how wonderfully our Lord always reached the sensitive core of men's hearts, and how expert under the tuition of the Holy Spirit, the disciples and apostles became in this same art of fitting their message to the need and condition of their hearers. Oh that we might learn it too!